DEATH IN THREE QUARTER TIME

A Collection of Short Stories

by

SIOUX DALLAS

CCB Publishing
British Columbia, Canada

Death in Three Quarter Time: A Collection of Short Stories

Copyright ©2009 by Sioux Dallas
ISBN-13   978-1-926585-26-0
First Edition

Library and Archives Canada Cataloguing in Publication

Dallas, Sioux, 1930-
Death in three quarter time: a collection of short stories /
written by Sioux Dallas – 1st ed.
ISBN 978-1-926585-26-0
I. Title.
PS3604.A439D42 2009   813'.6   C2009-903005-5

Publisher: CCB Publishing
             British Columbia, Canada
             www.ccbpublishing.com

To Robert Miles, Attorney at Law

You're the best boss in the world.

Contents

SHE WHO WAITS

The pain was cutting inside her like a wild animal tearing hungrily at raw meat. Sitting on a packing case, she rocked slowly back and forth, her arms wrapped across her stomach as if she needed to hold her insides in place.

"I'm worried to death about her. It's been almost two months and she isn't getting any better. Sometimes I despair that she will ever improve."

"She's your twin sister and she did come to you because she apparently felt the bond between you. She must have expected to get better by being with you, or maybe she thought, or hoped, you could make her better."

"I'm not sure she does expect help. We have been close, in fact we often felt each other's pain. Why didn't I discover this before it got so bad? I know I'm her comfort zone in an emotional storm."

"Don't sell yourself short. She blocked her troubles from you because she didn't want you suffering, too. You're doing a great job here. The natives are healthier and happier because of you."

Dr. Michael Bolling's heart was breaking for his twin, Dr. Verta Bolling Stallard. He drew a deep breath and turned to his assistant, Dr. Elaine Morris. Michael and Elaine had teamed for more than a year to bring medical care and nutrition as well as teaching sanitary practices to the people of Coiobo, Brazil. They worked as medical missionaries and had been satisfied with the response from the people.

Elaine was a widow and seventeen years older than Michael, so he had developed a close bond with her and an appreciation for her tenacity.

Elaine wished she could help, could do something, but what? "What caused her to be in this condition? The last I heard she had a successful practice as a beloved pediatrician in San Diego. I've wanted to ask but felt I should wait until you were ready to share. She talks to me and answers questions, but she is -- well, detached."

Michael sighed and sat on an upended barrel. He looked as if he wanted to cry. 'As you know Verta married Dr. Andrew Stallard, a very successful child psychologist. They were so much in love and never lost the first glow of love. They both wanted children, but it just didn't seem to be in the cards. Finally, after six years of marriage, they got pregnant. You have never seen two people more jubilant."

"How wonderful. It's great when parents really want children and will love and care for them. They truly must have been ecstatic."

"They were. And, believe it or not, they were more in love than ever, and they both adored that little boy, Andrew, Jr. They didn't want him to be called Junior, so they called him Butch."

"You're talking in the past tense. Where are her husband and child?" Elaine saw the grieved expression on Michael's face. "Oh, dear, I have a sinking feeling that the rest of the story will not be pleasant."

"There was an outbreak of some child's disease, and Verta was on duty at the hospital for three days. Verta didn't want to risk carrying germs home to her baby, so she slept at the hospital. She phoned Andrew as often as she could and finally told him the outlook was better. Andrew brought fifteen months old, Butch, to the hospital to see his mother."

Here Michael hung his head and was silent for a moment. Elaine could tell it was a painful telling for him. He continued talking without raising his head.

"No one knew that a man had entered the hospital carrying a pistol. The man's wife had died after an auto accident, and he blamed the hospital. He was grieving his loss because his wife was carrying their first child. He especially blamed the woman doctor who had cared for his wife. Verta was not the woman doctor, but all the grieving man could see was a woman doctor."

"Oh, dear. I know I'm not going to like hearing this." Elaine spoke softly.

"I sure didn't like hearing it," Michael said through tight lips. "I couldn't get away in time to be there and give her the support during the double funeral."

"Double funeral! Sorry, please go on. What happened?"

The man looked at Verta and leveled his pistol at her. Andrew saw him and without thinking, with all the love in his heart, threw himself in front of Verta. He still had Butch, little Andy, in his arms. The first bullet went through Butch and into Andrew. The next two killed them both. They fell at Verta's feet. She was so covered in blood from hugging them, the hospital staff thought she was wounded. They had to forcibly take her away. She was given a sedative and put to bed."

"Security had been called when the man was first observed in the lobby, but they were too late to save Verta's husband and child. She went into a world of her own to shut out the sight of what she had witnessed. She had no interest in reality. Oh, she had short periods of awareness and rationality, but for the most part, she wouldn't allow herself to feel or think."

"Why did she come here to the jungle? I would think this would be a difficult adjustment for her."

"Andrew's parents have been taking care of her. They loved her and, even with their own loss and grief, brought her to live with them. When they realized she wasn't showing improvement and was sinking deeper in herself, they thought it might help her to be with me. So they sent her here."

"As much as my heart aches for her, Michael, we have our work and we must continue. These people are depending on us. Hopefully, being here with missionary doctors will help Verta to return to reality and again take joy in her work."

"I hope we're ready. Here comes a chief with a long line of women and children. Dear God. Look at the condition of most of these children. Sticks for arms and legs and bloated stomachs. Between malnutrition, war between tribes, unsanitary conditions and every disease one can think of, these precious little fellows don't stand a chance in life."

"And the majority of the women are pregnant. Sometimes I feel as if we're spinning our wheels to try to teach them birth control, nutrition and cleanliness." Elaine sighed.

"Look at this," Mike spoke as if he were going to cry. "I thought we'd seen everything. This little one is probably just barely a year old and he looks like a dried up little old man. Hey! His mother is going into labor. We have one to deliver," he called excitedly. "Here, Verta. Do me a favor. Hold this little one while I deliver his sibling."

Verta didn't have time to think about it. Mike laid the baby on her lap and turned quickly to take care of the mother. He had laid the mother on a canvas cot and was trying to work with her.

Verta stared at the little brown baby. Her body straightened and she began to shake. The baby gave a pitiful cry, but was so weak that he had no energy to do as normal children would. Verta kept looking at him as if he were a coiled snake ready to strike.

Michael glanced at her every chance he got. *Will she touch the baby, or will she fall apart? How long is she going to just sit there?*

After a few minutes, that seemed longer than they were, Verta timidly touched the tiny hand. She picked him up and cuddled him in her arms. She finally looked up to see Elaine looking at her. "Elaine, do we have food supplies for a baby --and diapers?"

"Some," Elaine answered quickly, too busy to stop. "Look on the table in the tent behind you." She gave a sigh of relief when Verta looked interested.

Verta got up slowly, cuddling the little boy as if she were afraid he would break. She came out of the tent in a few minutes giving him a bottle of special formula. She had washed him and put a diaper on him.

"Don't give him too much at once," Michael called to her. "His stomach won't take it. In fact, he would get sick because he isn't accustomed to good food."

"I know," Verta answered with no expression. "I only have three ounces in the bottle."

"Good. When you finish feeding him, would you please help with some of these children. There's so many of them. A hug and a smile will go a long way with all of them."

For almost three hours Michael and Elaine worked nonstop with the large group. All of them needed medical attention, adults and children. There were open sores on women's feet and legs from various injuries. There were stings and insect bites of all kinds and a skin rash that was difficult to diagnose. None of the women could say where they contacted the rash. Michael called Elaine's attention to the large number of venereal diseases.

Michael was happy to see that Verta was showing some interest in the baby. She had fed him and diapered him again. She ignored everyone and everything around her except the little boy.

"What a day," Michael gasped. "It was satisfying in a way, and so depressing, too, when we don't seem to be making much progress teaching these people. They walk for miles to come to us for help, and then go back to their own village and live the same deplorable way they've been living."

Elaine stretched and rubbed the small of her back. "At least your sister showed some interest in the little boy. I thought that she wasn't gong to give the baby back to his mother at first. She seemed astonished that the mother stood up holding her newborn and reached to carry the little boy.

I thought she was going to run after them when they walked back into the jungle." She sighed. "I'm going to the river for a bath." Elaine gathered soap, towels and a change of clothes.

Michael assigned two husky young men, who carried rifles, to walk with her and keep an eye out for trouble. There were not only unfriendly people, but snakes and a variety of wild animals that might prove dangerous. He knew the guards would be respectful to her and protect her.

For several weeks the missionary camp was busy almost every day as group after group came for help. Sometimes the chief, or head of the group, needed medical attention, but most of them stood rigidly and watched.

On Sunday Michael played his guitar and sang with the people who would attend his talks. He would tell them Bible stories and encouraged each one to have trust in Christ. Elaine taught the children songs and told them Bible stories that they could understand. Much to their delight, Verta started helping

Thursday, of that week, they were not as busy as they had been. Elaine was taking inventory of medical supplies so they could send requests to the home office for what they needed. "Michael, your sister seems to her old self. She's been a valuable worker with the children and she even smiles and laughs with them."

"I know. There's something in her eyes though, or rather, there's nothing there at times. It's as if she has no life. Or maybe as if she's waiting for something important to happen."

"Give her time, Michael. She had a serious, traumatic shock, not only losing her husband and child, but seeing them die right before her eyes. And all that blood. She *is* a doctor and could do nothing to save them. Don't you imagine she blamed herself for not saving them? She is getting better, slowly but surely."

Hearing a sound from the path in the jungle, Elaine looked up to see a man with several women and loads of children coming into their camp. She could tell by the position of the women that the man considered all the women as wives. They were in a single line staying right behind him. "Michael," she called shocked. "That's a white man. Look how he's hitting those poor women, treating them as slaves. It's obvious he doesn't have any care for the children. See the fear on their faces."

"I see what he's doing. I can't treat him as I would love to do so. Remember, our job is to treat illnesses and share the truth of salvation with the people. We might get through to most of the children, but the women are too frightened to listen. I can tell that man is not going to be receptive to anything except free help. He probably doesn't care whether his people receive treatment or not. He has just come to us out of curiosity. He probably doesn't see white people more than a couple of times a year. "

The two doctors worked quickly with the injuries, some of them obviously abuse from this man. They tried to be friendly but the women seemed afraid to smile or talk. They tried to make the children smile, but they only looked afraid.

The children looked to the man for permission to accept candy sticks given to them. They would grab a stick and scuttle behind their mother. It was unnerving to work in the silence of the group.

The man sat on a barrel, smoking a pipe, and staring at the doctors.

To help them through the silence, Elaine had played some tapes of gospel songs. Michael was bending over a little girl cutting a long thorn that had been embedded in her thigh. He jerked with shock when the white man gave a scream of surprise. Michael whirled to see Verta level a rifle and blast the man's stomach full of holes. The women screamed and ran back into the jungle, dragging frightened children with them. A lot of them still needed treatment.

For a moment Michael could not make himself move. Elaine was frozen in shock. By the time Michael could dive for Verta and knock the rifle from her hands, it was too late. The man was dead.

"I knew I'd get him," Verta gave a chilling smile. "I just waited and asked God to send him to me."

"Verta, do you know this man?"

She nodded as if in a trance, still smiling weirdly, but her eyes held no expression. "Yes, he's the one who killed my love. That's the main reason I was willing to come here when Dad Stallard suggested it. That piece of filth escaped when he was being transferred from one jail to another. I heard a detective tell my in-laws that he had escaped to South America." She then stood like a statue.

"Oh, Verta." Elaine put her arms around Verta and Michael put his arms around both women. They stood hugging and crying. Verta stood stiff and still as if she were asleep. "She must have found the rifle that we kept for protection from snakes. I hadn't even missed it," Elaine moaned.

"I have to report this," Michael dropped his arms and shuddered. "Get her!" Michael yelled as he ran past Elaine and caught Verta as she walked like a zombie into the jungle. "What can I do?" he sobbed. "Elaine, please make the call. I guess we should call headquarter first and let them suggest what our next move should be."

Elaine hurried into a service tent and prepared to make a radio call. "Sit tight," the man at headquarters told her. "I'll notify the authorities and make arrangements for the body to be picked up. May I speak to Michael and ask him what he's going to do about his sister?"

"I'll have Michael call you later. He has his hands full now taking care of his sister. She's retreated into a world that none of us can penetrate. He's afraid she'll walk into the jungle and be lost or injured. Signing off."

She hurried to tell Michael of the call. "We have to restrain her until we can get her to a hospital for professional help. Verta is not to blame. I can't imagine how I would feel to see someone I loved with my whole heart killed right in front of me, but I'm beginning to understand. My heart is breaking for her. And then she sat in the blood hugging them for several minutes. Her in-laws apparently loved her, but she didn't get the psychiatric help she desperately needed. Michael, I hope it isn't too late to get the help for her now."

"I agree. I'll ask for a replacement while I go to San Diego with her. I'll come back as soon as I can, but she's my first responsibility now. I won't leave her until I'm satisfied that she's getting the treatment she needs. Our parents died when we were thirteen and we were the only children. We've always had each other, and I'm *not* abandoning her." Michael spoke as if he were pleading a case in court.

"I understand and don't blame you. There are other missionary doctors a little over fifty miles from here. They have a bigger camp and more workers. I bet one of them would be glad to help me for a while until someone can come down from the states." Elaine spoke thoughtfully.

"I have a better idea. I'll call and ask permission to close for a couple of weeks. You can go back with us, obtain needed medical supplies, rest a while and return when you have an adequate assistant. I'd worry too much about you being here alone. These young men, who have been trained to help us, are good, but they *are* natives. You would be the outsider in the event of a tribal war or any unpleasant situation.'

"You're right, Michael. I'll welcome a chance to go to a beauty shop and relax. I love our work, but we have been here a little over two years and there's a lot to be desired."

Michael kept Verta sedated. Two days later they left with natives carrying Verta on a stretcher. After walking about six miles, they got on a truck that took them to Rio de Janeiro. There they took a plane to Brasilia and from there to San Diego. An ambulance was waiting for them and they went straight to a hospital where the staff was prepared and waiting to start work.

Two days later Dr. Chad Garrett met Michael for a conference. "I've examined your sister and have run extensive tests. I'm so sorry, but I can't offer much hope. Sometimes a patient will come out of this, but for the most part, they stay in a world that keeps them from the reality of life. Michael, you can't give up on your own life. You can't do a thing for her and you are needed badly where you've been working."

"My brain tells me you're right, but my heart won't let me leave my sister. My partner is going back with a man and wife team and a young man training for our work. I don't need to worry about the work, but my sister does need me."

"Why? We don't know that she can even hear you, and what good would it do for you to wear yourself out just sitting by her bed and looking at her?" Dr. Garrett asked kindly.

A month later, Michael kissed Verta's cheek and left her still staring into space. Time, medical help and unceasing prayer was what was needed. Verta's in-laws had volunteered to visit and be with her. Several nurses had volunteered to write and keep him informed as to what was happening.

Michael boarded the plane with a heavy heart, yet eager to get back to work. He put his head back against the seat, closed his eyes and whispered, "Lord, I'm placing my sister in your hands for You are the great Healer. You are far superior to any help that can be given to her here, but I know You'll work through the hands and skills of the hospital staff to do what is needed for Verta. Be with me, Lord, and be with us in our work."

Michael's eyes closed from emotional and physical exhaustion. As he slept, he gave a little smile as if he could see the ray of light that came through the window and gently touched him.

OUT OF TUNE

"You. Are. Drunk."

"No'm not. I don't think so," he giggled. He looked at his feet. "But the floor is sure unsteady. See. The floor's tilting." He giggled as he staggered around and tried to keep his balance.

"Number one, you're on board ship. Number two, **you are drunk!**" She almost screamed in her frustration.

"Am not," he continued to giggle. "Can't be. Just been sipping a little." He frowned and looked thoughtful. "Yeah. Been sipping."

"Well, you'd better stop sipping," she said sarcastically. "It's three o'clock and you have to play during the dinner seating starting at six. I hope you haven't drunk so much that you've forgotten, or won't be able to play."

"Forgotten what, my love?" He weaved and grinned, pushing his face close to hers. His wavy, blonde hair hung in disarray and the whites of his blue eyes were red and not well focused. He was five-ten with an average build, not very athletic, but was well known over the world for his artistry at the piano. He yawned and rubbed his eyes.

Her black eyes snapped as she tried to reason with him. Her black hair and olive skin showed Latin heritage as did her five-four slim build. "Don't my love me. The only reason we're on board is for us to take advantage of a cost-free cruise, which we badly need, in exchange for you playing through dinner and again in the lounge at nine each night.

"Oh, yeah." He fought to keep his balance as the ship swept over the leaping waves. The sky was darkening and the wind was rising. "Now love, you know I can play in my sleep," he snickered as he staggered away from her.

Turning to face her, and walking backwards, he tried to do a tap dance. Embarrassed, she dropped her head and walked on past him. A scream startled her. She looked back to see that her husband had fallen backwards over deck chairs where two horrified elderly ladies were seated.

"Why, that's Leo Worseck, the world-known pianist. What's wrong with him?" The ladies looked expectantly at her.

"I'm so sorry. Please forgive him. He's worked for several weeks without a break, and I'm afraid he's trying to take all those breaks on the same day," she tried to laugh, but it came out as a hollow sound.

"Who are you?" one of the ladies asked curiously.

"My name is Veronica. I'm Leo's wife. Again, forgive us." She hurried forward to catch up with her husband who had gotten up and staggered off.

"Sorry, darling, but the floor just won't stay still," he continued to giggle.

Veronica couldn't contain her tears and then looked ashamed as Purser Alan Weaver hurried toward them.

"May I be of assistance, Mrs. Worseck?" he asked pleasantly.

"Thank you, no. We're going straight to our cabin. Aren't we, darling?" she spoke firmly as she took Leo's arm to walk away.

Before Veronica could steady him, Leo pitched forward again and would have fallen flat on his face if Purser Weaver hadn't caught him.

"May I have the pleasure of walking to your cabin with you?" he asked politely.

"I would be grateful," Veronica said humbled. She caught her breath. "Oh, hello, Captain."

"Good afternoon. I hope you're enjoying the cruise. If there's anything we can do to make your trip more pleasant, we would appreciate the opportunity." Captain Adam Corbin smiled as he touched the brim of his cap with two fingers and walked on. Veronica, knew without a doubt, that he had observed her husband's failing, but he was a gentleman and left them in Purser Weaver's hands.

"Thank you so much," Veronica said sincerely as the Purser helped Leo into the cabin and led him to the bed.

"My pleasure, ma'am. I hope your husband can take a nap and feel better. He'll be more rested to play the piano tonight." He touched the brim of his cap and left.

Two hours later Veronica answered a knock at the door. "Hello, Captain. What is it?"

"I hope I'm not disturbing you, but I just came by to see if your husband is feeling better."

"I'm sure he will be. He's slept since we came to the cabin. I'm just preparing to get him up so he can shower, eat a bite and dress for his engagement. Thank you, Captain." She shut the door before anything else could be said. She looked at her husband with revulsion as she woke him.

Lightening flashed and thunder cracked and rolled as Leo and Veronica walked to the piano. A few diners, nearest the piano, recognized him and there was a scattering of applause.

A silence came over the room as he raised both hands and began a beautiful classical piece. He was truly gifted with great talent. As the night crept in, Leo played jazz and pop. Tired waiters attempted to encourage diners to leave so they could clear the tables and prepare for the next seating.

A few diners had bought drinks for Leo and left money in the tip jar on the piano. "Come back at nine for more listening pleasure and dancing," the diners were told.

Leo played as if he were matching the fury of the storm in its intensity. Banging the keys and throwing his head, his hair fell over his forehead and he became lost in the music.

Smiling, the Captain wove through the people and came to the piano. "Mr. Worseck, why don't you take a break and rest for your performance later," Captain Corbin suggest tactfully. Veronica whispered to him. Leo reluctantly stood and stomped away.

"Mrs. Worseck."

"Yes, Captain?"

"After you get your husband settled in your cabin, I would like for you to return and talk about something of importance. I won't keep you long."

"I shall return as quickly as possible," Veronica answered nervously and hurried to follow Leo to their cabin. She urged him to lie down and rest, assuring him that she would return and get him up in time for his late performance. It was now eight-twenty.

Captain Corbin courteously stood and held a chair for Veronica as she joined him.

"Thank you for being willing to talk to me, Mrs. Worseck. I have never enjoyed talking about unpleasant subjects, but, as Captain and an employee of the owners of the ship line, I have a duty."

"I understand," Veronica replied softly.

"Mrs. Worseck, it's obvious that Mr. Worseck is drinking more than he should. I'm sorry to bring up such a tender subject, but I've heard, and read, of his recent reputation. I know how brilliantly he has played for several years. Then, for some reason, he began drinking heavily, having fist fights, and -- uh-- was photographed with various very young, beautiful women, whom he was apparently escorting."

"Rich and spoiled women," Veronica snapped. "They chased after him."

"I don't doubt that they did. We agreed to allow him to play for this cruise as a favor to his brother."

"His brother! They haven't spoken in years. In fact, I've never met him."

"I know, but Gerald is one of the attorneys for this cruise line. He has kept up with you through news reports and mutual friends. He's aware of how you've struggled to help your husband and he asked us to do this as a favor to both of you. I must tell you that we can't allow the behavior Mr. Worseck exhibited today because we are responsible for the safety, and the happiness, of thousands of people on his ship. Do you think you can help him control himself for the two weeks we'll be out?"

"Oh, yes, Captain, I'm sure I can. Please give us another chance. I will promise that Leo will be a different person. You can rely on him."

"One more chance, Mrs. Worseck. I have to answer to others, therefore, I must be firm about the situation."

"I understand and I can't thank you enough for your kindness. If there's nothing else, I'm sure you'll excuse me. I must get back to the cabin and help Leo get ready."

The Captain stood as she jumped up and hurried away. His second in command, Ben Rapalsky, sat down in the chair Veronica had vacated. "Do you think she can keep him in line?"

"We'll let her try. I feel sorry for her," Captain Corbin answered.

The performance at nine started well. People called out requests and Leo played in his usual beautiful style, helping people to remember fondly the days gone by as well as songs of the present. Veronica sang some of the songs and encouraged the crowd to join in. Her professionally trained contralto voice was a delight. Some tunes, to dance by, brought sighs of remembrance and some caused hysterical laughter as those who didn't mind being a clown, showed off.

As the performance continued, people brought drinks for Leo and sat them on the piano. He drank greedily in spite of Veronica begging him not to. His tip glass was overflowing and Veronica had emptied it twice. As eleven rolled around, Leo was banging and yelling as he tried to sing. Captain Corbin called for two crew members to take Leo to his cabin. Veronica followed with her head down and visibly trying hard not to cry.

Forty-five minutes later, Captain Corbin called Ben over. "Please go to the Worseck cabin and inquire if Mrs. Worseck needs anything."

"I shall be glad to, sir."

As Ben started down the stairs to the lower deck, he saw two shapes of people at the rail. One shape bent over and the second shape flipped over the rail into the ocean.

"Man overboard!" he yelled as he ran to the spot. "Mrs. Worseck," he exclaimed in surprise as he recognized her.

Veronica, crying and moaning, was inconsolable. "My husband was unsteady and too inebriated to be out of the cabin. After we got to the cabin he insisted on coming back to play again. I guess he lost his balance in the storm. The ship was tossing wildly." She cried copious tears as the ship was stopped and searchlights were played on the water.

After the ship had turned around and gone back to the spot where the person had gone overboard, the crew could see a body floating on the leaping waves. They were able to snag the body and bring it up. Leo Worseck would play no more. The ship's doctor gave Veronica a shot to calm her and help her sleep.

The next morning Captain Corbin introduced Veronica to Leo's brother. "Gerald flew in this morning by helicopter," the Captain explained to the astonished Veronica. "We had to notify headquarters of the loss."

Gerald reached to hug Veronica. "I'm truly sorry that we meet for the first time like this, and I'm more sorry to inform you that you're under arrest for the murder of your husband -- my brother," he spoke sadly.

"Murder!" she screamed out. "How can you say that? All of you know how much I cared for Leo and gave up my career to help him. How can you? All of you know how much he had drunk and wasn't able to walk." She collapsed in tears.

"Mrs. Worseck, I want you to hear what these men have to say." The Captain placed a hand on her shoulder and urged her to sit back down. "These are the two men who took your husband to your cabin last night."

"I'm sorry ma'am, but we have to tell the truth," one man stated.

"Truth? What are you saying? You brought him to the cabin and left."

"Yes, ma'am. We took him in, undressed him down to his shorts and put him to bed. He was passed out cold."

"Yes," the Captain continued, "when his body was brought up, he was fully dressed, shoes tied and even a shirt and tie on."

"I told you he was determined to return to the lounge and continue playing."

The Captain shook his head sadly. "He was too drunk to have dressed so completely. Even if he'd awakened on his own, he might have put on pants, but he wouldn't have dressed as completely as he was. You roused him and dressed him to go out to the rail where you could -- uh -- help him overboard. Didn't you?"

"No! No! Why would I hurt him? I've stood by him through all the years of heartaches and triumphs -- and --"

Ben knelt in front of her, speaking softly. "Mrs. Worseck, I came to see if I could do anything to help you. When I saw one human form go over the rail, I realized that one person had pushed the other one over. I was flabbergasted to find you. When the body was brought up, fully dressed, I knew I was right; I had witnessed a murder."

"Do you blame me?" she screamed, jumping up to pace. "This was our last chance and he was ruining it, as usual." She spit out the words.

Gerald placed an arm across her shoulders. "I do understand how frustrated you might feel, but there's no excuse for taking another person's life."

Veronica spoke through wrenching sobs. "I shouldn't talk harshly about my husband. The truth is, I've always covered for him. Everyone knows I'm six years older than Leo. I knew he was attracted to me, but he would never have married me if I had not been rich. It didn't take long for him to run through the fortune my grandfather left me. He flirted with women, but I ignored it because he always came home to me. Two years ago he met a wealthy, lovely young woman by the name of Chariese Kennedy. Word got back to me that he offered to divorce me if she would marry him. She refused, but he wouldn't let her alone. Her brother hired two men to beat him so badly that his hands were injured. He couldn't play for a while and lost a great job with the Boston Symphony. Our savings were soon gone. This was our last chance to get him started again on a legitimate round of appearances."

"And knowing there would be no income, the two million dollars insurance policy looked mighty good," Gerald said.

"How did you know about that?"

"My little brother might not have kept in touch because he didn't want big brother advising him, but that didn't mean I wouldn't keep track of him."

"I deserve the money. He had wasted mine and had used me for seven years. I'm thirty-nine and I deserve a life without --" she collapsed in deep sobs.

Captain Corbin took her hands and spoke with compassion. "Mrs. Worseck, we all agree that you had a tragic marriage. You know what's really sad?" She looked at him through tear-filled eyes.

"Yesterday morning I heard you playing and singing in the lounge before others came in. I remembered you had a promising career and gave it up to support your husband. I intended to contact the administrators and ask if I could offer the job to you. You would have had your career again and an income that you had earned. But -- you jumped the gun and now you must face the music.

WHAT'S IN A NAME

Cornelia Martin rubbed her distended stomach with a joyous smile. Two more weeks and her baby would be in her arms, the baby that she and Dale had loved from conception and wanted with all their hearts. She didn't mind that her ankles were swollen and she could hardly walk without staggering and the ever loving waddle. Sometimes her whole body ached until she could not sleep. Even if she could sleep her stomach got in the way of lying in a comfortable position.

She fussed at herself as the phone rang across the room. Why hadn't she remembered to bring the cordless phone with her and have it close? The doctor had warned her that it was important to be alert because the baby might arrive earlier than expected.

Hurrying as well as she could, she hoped it was Dale saying that he could come home sooner than he thought. He was with a Marine group that had orders to ship overseas, but he had applied for special permission to be home for the birth of his first baby. Cornelia was an orphan and his family was too far away to get to her quickly. She only had Dale and he was praying he could be with her. Finally she reached the phone.

"Hello," she said breathlessly and eagerly. "Oh, hello, Belinda. No, I'm glad you called. I keep hoping to hear from Dale. What's going on in your life?" The chat lasted about fifteen minutes, ten minutes more than Cornelia wanted it to last. "I'm sorry, Belinda, but I must hang up. The throne room is calling me urgently. You know how that is with us pregnant ladies."

She cut the phone off and took it with her to the bathroom. She looked at her swollen face in the mirror. Fortunately she was blessed with a clear, creamy complexion. Curly copper-colored hair hung listlessly and beautiful, almost jade-colored eyes looked tired, which she was. She sighed heavily and waddled out of the bathroom with the intention of going to her bedroom and lying down. A knock at the back door took her in that direction.

"Well, Adrienne, what a nice surprise. I haven't seen you for a few days and wondered if you hadn't gone to your mother's for a visit. Come on in and we'll have a cup of tea. I'm so tired all of the time, and as much as I'm loving being pregnant, I want to be able to hold my baby and wear pretty clothes again. I'd also love to be able to look down and see my feet." They both laughed.

"Go lie down and I'll make the tea and bring cups for both of us. Bryan had to go out of town on a business trip and I've been getting clothes ready and running errands for him. He's been a veritable slave driver because he's so anxious to make good. There's a promotion dangling in front of him like the proverbial carrot. At last he's gone and I can draw a relieved breath." She crossed her fingers and her eyes to draw a laugh from Cornelia.

Gratefully Cornelia waddled back to her bedroom and thanked her lucky stars to have a neighbor like Adrienne. If Dale couldn't make it in time, maybe Adrienne would go to the hospital with her. *Why hasn't Dale called? Oh, I hope there's no cog in the wheel and he can be here for me and the baby. I'm anxious to know whether it's a boy or girl. We both wanted to wait and be surprised. We'll both love whatever it is.*

"Thank you, Adrienne. What a sweetheart you are, and you even brought cookies. I'm loving, and craving, all kinds of sweet things, but I promise that I'll diet and exercise like crazy just as soon as I can after the baby joins our family."

"Have you decided on a name? You know a name is very important. What does Dale's family think of this since he's the oldest and the only one married? Are any of his family coming to see you?"

"Whoa," Cornelia laughed. "I can only answer one question at a time. Name? We haven't really decided on one yet. We'll make that decision together. We want a name that will mean something and sound important when the child is grown and working. Dale's family is ecstatic. All of them call frequently and want to be here for the big event, but coming from Alaska to Florida is a mighty long trip. You know that his father is career Army and is stationed in Alaska. Dale is twenty-four, his twenty year old brother, Nicholas, is in college in Washington. His seventeen year old sister, Daphne, is finishing high school and preparing to go to college and his fifteen year old brother, Malcolm, is only thinking of football and girls. Dale's mother is so anxious to be here, for her first grandchild, but she has a lot of people depending on her there.

"It must be nice to have so many in a family and they seem to be so close. They seem to love each other so much and enjoy being a family. Oh, dear. I'm sorry, Cornelia. For a moment I didn't remember that you were an only child and both of your parents died a few years ago. I'm sorry. Sometimes my mouth starts running and I can't find a brake."

"Don't worry about it. I'm accustomed to being alone. Dale and I met in college and he joined the Marines soon after we were married. I've traveled around so much that I'm glad to have this apartment until Dale can come home and we can buy a house. We want more children and some day I'll put my teaching certificate to work." Cornelia groaned and held her back. She tried to roll to her right side and ended in an awkward position, laughing until tears rolled down her cheeks. "I'm an elephant," she laughed.

"Here, let me give you a back massage." Adrienne hurried to the far side of the bed and sat on it. She rubbed Cornelia's back and had her laughing telling about the people who came into the county clerk's office where she worked. "There now. Maybe you can relax and take a nap. Enjoy naps while you can; there'll soon be a siren keeping you awake and demanding attention. Do you want me to check on you later?"

"Thank you so much. I do feel better. No, I'm going to take a hot shower, eat a sandwich and read in bed until I fall asleep. Oh, please let me hear from Dale."

Adrienne found a soft, white nightgown for Cornelia and checked to make sure there were towels and shampoo in the bathroom. She also checked to make sure the shower mat was in place and wouldn't be slippery. She offered to stay until Cornelia had her shower but Cornelia thanked her and refused.

Dale's parents called faithfully every night. Adrienne called each day to offer to get groceries or run errands. Cornelia felt so blessed, but why hadn't she heard from Dale except that one letter saying that he would be permitted to come home. She expected him any day.

One night when Alicia Martin, Dale's mother, had called to chat with Cornelia, she was distressed to hear that Cornelia's back kept hurting and she was having to urinate so often. "Honey, that's a sign the baby has dropped and is ready to greet the world. I'm trying very hard to get away from here and be there with you no later than three days from now. Be brave. We all love you and feel so blessed to have you in our family."

On a Thursday afternoon Cornelia was napping when a noise at the bedroom door alerted that someone was there. She opened her eyes to see Adrienne's black hair sneak around the door and one dark brown eye peek at her. When Adrienne saw that Cornelia was awake, she came on in bringing a crisp, fresh smell of early November air, cool but not yet cold, and a promise of rain in the air.

"Hey, slug-a-bed," Adrienne called. "I came to see if you would join me in a cup of tea."

Cornelia laughed until she could hardly sit on the side of the bed. "We wouldn't have fit in a cup before I was pregnant and now there's no chance of it."

Adrienne knelt to put Cornelia's house slippers on her and then helped her to stand. They went to the kitchen where Adrienne had left a fresh-baked lemon pound cake on the table. The warm lemony smell was irresistible. They drank tea, ate cake and laughed and chatted until five o'clock.

Cornelia kept rubbing her back and saying what weird pains she was having. She told Adrienne what her mother-in-law had said about hurting low in the back was a sign the baby might be dropping.

Adrienne suddenly stood up and apologized for keeping Cornelia up so long. She asked if there was anything she could do for Cornelia and left in a flurry calling back, "Bye now. I'm going to beat the rain home. Call me if you need anything."

Cornelia shuddered when the cold rain began to beat against the window as if something was knocking to be let in. Darkness fell early. She scolded herself again when the phone rang in the other room and she had trouble getting up from the kitchen chair. The pain in her back sent her screaming down on the chair again. She was hurting so much that she rolled from the chair and to the floor. Her stomach was twisting and turning as if a knife was cutting through her.

"Dear, Lord, the baby is coming and I can't even get to the phone. Oh, Adrienne, where are you? Dale, where are **you**?" she screamed.

The kitchen door opened letting in the cold, wet air. Adrienne stood there in a black raincoat looking as if she were on a fishing boat. She had a wide-brimmed black hat of the same material as the coat and a pair of knee length black rubber boots.

"Oh, Adrienne. You're an angel. I think the baby is coming. Please hurry and call the hospital, ask for an ambulance and tell them to call my doctor." She paused for

29

another pain and a scream. "Get my bag out of the closet in my bedroom and my raincoat."

Cornelia looked puzzled when Adrienne just stood smiling at her and saying nothing. She walked over to look down at Cornelia. "I knew it wouldn't be long. Dale doesn't really want this baby or he would be here, and you're too young, and inexperienced, to know how to care for one."

"Too young? I'm twenty-three and what does any of that have to do with this. Of course Dale wants our baby. Adrienne, what's the matter with you. Why are you acting so strange? You're frightening me." She gave another gasp and huffed and puffed with the pain.

"I'll love this baby and care for it as if it were my own. I've been seeing about you because I wanted to be sure my baby was being taken care of properly." Adrienne said solemnly.

"Your baby," Cornelia whispered confused. Then looking straight into Adrienne's eyes, she saw the strange expression, and, to her horror, realized Adrienne's mind was sick.

"Yes. You see I didn't tell you that Bryan left me for another woman, one that was carrying his baby. If I have a baby, he'll come back to me."

Cornelia screamed in pain and in fright.

"Hush," Adrienne ordered her, kneeling on the floor beside her. She took her hands out of her pockets and reached behind her where she was carrying a back pack. She opened the pack on the floor beside Cornelia. In the pack were clean, soft cloths, baby oil, diapers and baby clothes.

Cornelia couldn't keep from screaming. Adrienne put her hand over her mouth. "Don't make a noise. Someone might hear you and come to see what's going on."

Adrienne kept one hand over Cornelia's mouth as she pulled Cornelia's gown up to see if the baby was being born. It seemed like hours as they were there with Adrienne's hand over Cornelia's mouth and Cornelia screaming with pain after pain with contractions.

Cornelia's eyes opened wide with fright as Cornelia reached into the pack and held up a sharp knife. "It's taking too long. I guess I'd better cut it out and take off before someone comes in."

Taking her hand from Cornelia's mouth, she reached to raise the dress higher, holding the knife ready to be used. Cornelia tried to fight her but the pains were too severe. She drew in such a sharp breath that it choked her when Adrienne placed the knife high on Cornelia's stomach and drew it down toward the legs.

"Adrienne, I thought we were friends. You said we are like sisters. How can you do this? You'll kill me and maybe kill my baby."

"**My baby!**" Adrienne screamed and placed the knife to cut deeper.

At that moment the door flew open and a male voice shouted, 'What's going on here?"

Adrienne sprang up and held the knife to attack the man. He was in shock but quickly saw a stack of clean dishtowels on the kitchen table. He grabbed a couple and wrapped them around his left arm. He then thrust his arm toward her and at the same time kicked her in the stomach. She screamed in anger and bent over. Taking advantage of this, he kicked her hand holding the knife and saw it spin away across the kitchen floor. Making a fist he came up hard under her chin and laid her out cold.

He quickly tore a towel in strips and bound her hand and ankles. Turning to look at Cornelia on the floor, he cried out in grief to see the wound on her stomach bleeding and the tip of a tiny head trying to be born. Afraid that the baby would die, he ran into the living room and frantically found the phone. Dialing 911 he told the operator to send an ambulance and the police. He then ran back into the kitchen and gathered Cornelia in his arms.

Cornelia gained conscientiousness as the sirens came blaring in front of the apartment. The paramedics placed a compress on Cornelia's wound. They quickly took stats and called them in to the hospital giving information that was needed. They quickly placed her on a collapsed gurney and lifted it to wheel it out.

The police took custody of Adrienne but the man could not tell them who she was or why she was there. "I just came in to see her with a knife trying to cut the baby out of Cornelia's stomach."

He insisted that he be allowed to go with Cornelia. "Are you the father?" a paramedic asked.

"No. I'm Nicholas Martin, her brother-in-law. She's married to my brother who is in the Marines. Oh, it's a long story and you're wasting time. I am going to the hospital and if you want to talk to me, follow me there, or better still, take me there."

Cornelia had a strong, healthy boy born in the ambulance. The doctor was worried because of the trauma the mother had gone through just as he was being born. He wasn't sure if this would have an adverse effect on the baby. But Cornelia had been so healthy and happy while she was carrying him that he was fine.

The next morning Cornelia awakened to find a rumpled Nicholas in a chair by her bed. He had slept in his clothes and needed a shave. He had defied the nurses and stayed by Cornelia all night. They could have had him arrested but the doctor said that, under the circumstances, hospital rules could be bent a little. He said both Cornelia and Nicholas would be relieved to be together.

It was natural that Cornelia was concerned about Dale and why Nicholas had left college to come to her. Her guardian angel had surely brought him at just an opportune time. "I prayed all the way," he kept saying. The next day Alicia and David Martin arrived.

Cornelia was even more concerned about Dale and why her parents-in-law had come and her brother-in-law, but no husband.

Alicia told her story first. "I knew when I talked to you on the phone that the baby was on the way. That same day we got a call that Dale had been in an accident and was in the hospital. He didn't want them to call you, knowing your condition, so he had them call us. I wanted to come that minute, but couldn't get away."

David broke in, "I wired money to Nicholas and ask him to please be here for you. From what I've heard, he arrived like he might have been in a movie suspense drama. He could not have timed it better if he'd planned it."

"I almost fainted from shock when I saw that woman with a bloody knife in her hand and realized that Cornelia was on the floor at her feet bleeding. I didn't know whether you were still alive or what was happening," he told Cornelia. "I didn't have time to plan. I just acted by instinct and protected my arm from the knife while I tried to get her away from you."

Three nurses had stood by to hear the story. "God was sure with you," one of them stated.

Another one snapped, "Well. If God was with her why did He cause this to happen to her in the first place?"

The third one spoke. "God doesn't cause things like this to happen. Besides, if we knew all the answers we'd be as knowledgeable as God and that's not possible. Yes. He **was** with her or help would not have arrived in time."

The doctor nodded his head and asked everyone to leave the room so he could examine Cornelia and talk with her.

Two days later Cornelia had just finished nursing the baby when the Martin family came in for another visit and to cuddle the very welcome member of the family. The door of her room opened and all looked to see who was entering. Alicia gave a cry and handed the baby to David who immediately handed him to Nicholas who laid him beside Cornelia.

Dale stood on crutches with one leg in a full cast and bandages on his shoulder, neck and around his head. He hugged his parents and brother while pushing his way to the bed so he could hug his wife. "Oh, my darling, my joy, my breath, my heart, my love, my life, I've been in misery that I could not be here with you. If I had known what you were going through, I would have been out of my mind." He clumsily got on the bed beside her so that he could hug her better.

Finally Dale looked up with tears in his eyes. "Nicholas, from what I can understand, you saved the life of my darling wife and my precious son. I can never thank you enough."

"No thanks necessary. I'm thankful I was there when I was. Why don't you get acquainted with your son," he placed the baby on Dale's chest.

"Let's all go down to the cafeteria and I'll treat everyone to a coffee and let this little family have some time alone." Nicholas moved everyone ahead of him as they reluctantly left.

"Where were you?" Cornelia asked in concern. "I wondered why I wasn't hearing from you. What happened to you?"

"Sweetheart, I was rushing to the plane. Lt. Jakobson was driving, and a drunk ran a red light and broadsided us right into my side. I was in the hospital for two days before I gained conscientiousness. Jakobson wasn't so lucky. He died during the night from internal injuries. I had the military chaplain call mom and dad and ask them not to tell you yet. I was afraid that you might have birth complications or try to come to me when it was time for this rascal to be born," he grinned down with pride at the tiny boy.

"He looks like me," he gloated.

Cornelia laughed. "I hope he grows up to look like you and to be a man such as you are."

Soon Nicholas and his parents were back in the room.

"Okay," Nicholas smiled. "I'd like to know what you're going to name this champion. And don't you dare even think of sticking that poor innocent baby with my name."

"Owen is Welsh for 'a warrior'," David said. "I've always liked the name."

"I like it," Cornelia clapped her hands.

Nicholas laughed. "You could call him Corny after his mother."

"Shut your mouth," Dale laughed. "If you won't call her by her full name, Cornelia, then call her Nelia." Turning to Cornelia he asked, "Did I ever tell you what Nicholas told the teacher about his dad's name when he entered kindergarten?' She shook her head and the family laughed. "We had just moved to Tucson and we were new to the community. The teacher asked Nicholas his name and then his mother's name. He told her it was mommy. She asked him what his daddy's name was and he said, daddy. She said, well, what does your mother call your daddy. Nothing, Nicholas said. She don't call him nothing cause she likes him."

David said, "How about Nicholas Owen Martin and call him Owen?"

Dale and Cornelia looked at each other and shook their heads.

The next day the family came to tell Dale and Cornelia that Nicholas and David were leaving but Alicia would stay to help. They were told that Cornelia would go home the next day. She had twenty-two stitches in her stomach because of the knife wound, but she was doing well. They were also told that the baby had been named.

Dale leaned against a chair and proudly held his son. Folks, I would like to introduce you to Dale Anthony Martin, Jr. I hesitated to agree to that because my initials spell D A M and I didn't want my son to go through life with that. Cornelia says we can call him Tony and people won't pay any attention to the initials.

The family applauded and kissed and hugged everyone around. Alicia hugged Cornelia and whispered. "I volunteered to stay but your husband is sure he can take care of everything. His dad has hired a nurse to come in during the day for two weeks to give you a chance to rest and to help keep Dale off his feet a little until he heals more. That head injury is nothing to sneeze at. I'll return just as soon as I can if you ever need me."

With tears coursing down her cheeks, Cornelia kissed Alicia's cheek and hugged her. "Thank you. I couldn't have had a better mother."

Dale hugged all of them and thanked them for coming. He kept hugging Nicholas and saying how much he appreciated him. "Before I go back on duty, this little family of mine will have a house and a fenced-in yard. I hope all of you will come as often as you can. Give Daphne and Malcolm my love. You have some pictures, but we'll send pictures often to show you how he's growing."

Cornelia winked at Nicholas. "And I'll be sure he knows his daddy's name before he starts school."

Nicholas grinned and held up his thumb in an okay sign. *I wonder if I should tell them that I looked in a book of names at the library and Adrienne is a French name meaning dark and foreboding?*

WHAT COMES AROUND

Scotland, 1497

Fortune Rutherford hurried along the narrow cobblestone street dodging the refuse being emptied from the windows of the homes above the street. Houses were built right on the street and the upstairs windows were hanging over the street.

Sniffing the air filled with moist breezes bringing the rain, she tried to get home before the storm struck. It was difficult to walk faster because her stomach was so big now that it made her clumsy. She rubbed her stomach smiling, "Ach, little one, yer mooch awaited."

The castle was just a short walk away around the copse and then she could cross the drawbridge to be safely home. Fortune loved her home and her husband, Baron Robert Rutherford, who was so dear to her heart. *Of course this wee bairn will be loved and cherished by both o us. This moost be a fine son I'm carrying because I'm so big. I moost hurry for Robert will be haime from his trip soon. I do hope Robert doesn't find that I went to the market alone. He is so fearful for me when I go oot withoot a guard or maid.*

Thankfully Fortune walked across the drawbridge just as the rain started. She hurried upstairs to change clothes before Robert would be home.

That evening Robert was waiting anxiously for Fortune in the dining room. It was their first wedding anniversary and Fortune's seventeenth birthday. Robert felt he was the richest man on earth; a beautiful, young wife, a baby due in a fortnight and blessings too numerous to count.

"Robbie, cariad (darling)," Fortune cried as she swept across the room and into his waiting arms. "I've been so alone withoot ye. Please tell me yer gae'n (you are going) to be haime (home) for the birth of our bairn (baby)."

"Aye, ghraidh mo chridhe (sweetheart of my heart), I'll be here. I have a gift fer ye," he spoke lovingly as he took something from his pocket.

She gasped. "Me hoisband! Where did ye foind such beautiful jewels? Thank ye, me cariad. How thoughtful o ye to present me with me birthstone. The amethyst and diamond earrings are just right."

"I had them made special fer ye, the moost beautiful mother-to-be in all the land. That's not all. Mayhap (maybe) ye'll like this." He reached into another pocket and brought out a matching necklace of amethyst and diamonds. "These are for the heir yer given me. I'm sure twill be a man child. No woman could be that large with a mere girl.

Laughing she fell into his arms for a kiss and a passionate embrace. Even though their marriage had been arranged by their parents, no two people could be more in love than Robert and Fortune.

In the middle of the night, Robert was awakened by moans and groans from Fortune. She was so wet with perspiration that the bedclothes were damp. His heart was heavy with terror as he bellowed for one of the maids to attend her.

Greeting the day the next morning was a proud Baron Robert Rutherford holding twin boys so that the staff could admire them. "Meet Andrew and Angus; Andrew being the oldest and the next Baron. Here, take them," he ordered a wet nurse. "Ye'll need to foind anither woman to help ye. Guard me sons with yer loife and I weel promise that yer oild age will be joyous and free from worry."

"Oh, me laird, they are beautiful and such braw bairns. I weel guard them wee me loife and I'll be sure anyone who helps me weel do the same. How is our dear lady?"

"Quite well considering that she had twins. Och, I knew that stomach was big for something grand," he laughed and the staff laughed and cheered. "She is so young, but she is me little warrior."

The nurse and a chosen maid went to the room prepared for a nursery. The remainder of the staff left to do their assigned work.

The next afternoon, Robert sat admiring his wife while she slept. Maids had brought them a platter of fruit, nuts, jams and scones with wine for a light lunch. Fortune was asleep before the food was cleared from the room. Robert was relaxing and almost asleep.

Robert's head jerked up hearing a noise that filled his heart with dread. They were under attack! How had this happened? Where were the guards at the drawbridge and where were the knights?

"Guards! Coom now and see to yer lady. I'll check on the ones who are supposed to be defending the castle. The ones who left the drawbridge down and unguarded will forfeit their loives." He was too late.

Before Robert could leave Fortune's bed chamber, and before his guards reached them, his arch enemy, Lord Ian

MacMurray, strode into the room followed by at least a dozen of his men.

"Weel, guid dai (well, good day) to ye, friend Robbie. How koind (kind) o ye to make open yer haime to me."

"The dai yer welcome in this haime, Ian MacMurray, weel be the end o toime (time). Me guid wife delivered twin bairns yesterday and she does not need to be disturbed."

"Och, I would love to disturb her," Ian swaggered toward the bed. Fortune awakened confused and angry.

"Leave her," Robert roared. He jumped at Ian but four of Ian's men bore him to the floor.

"Och, look at the pretty jewels. Me guid woife will certainly loive(love) me fer bringing them haime to her."

"Ye'll no touch me with yer filthy hands. Nor weel yer slut o a woife every enjoy them," Fortune yelled as she struggled to rise.

Ian laughed loudly. "I don't remember asking yer permission, me lady," he said mockingly as he made a facetious bow.

Robert screamed with anger and grief as Ian raised his sword and cut off Fortune's ears to take the earrings and then coldly cut off her head to take the necklace. Whipping around, he held the blade at Robert's throat.

Robert's gray eyes blazed in anger as he spoke. "I curse ye and all yer kin, Ian MacMurray. Any relative, or so called friend, o yers who possess this jewelry weel answer to me."

Ian threw his head back and laughed maniacally as he plunged the blade into Robert's chest. He calmly wiped the blade on Robert's shirt and strode out of the room, not realizing that Robert still lived.

Late in their arrival, but still effective, the guards killed many of the intruders and sent Ian MacMurray running. Even though the castle was now safe, there was a lot of damage to repair and much mourning as bodies were taken out to be buried.

The wet nurse, two maids and two guards had hidden with the babies. There was loud wailing and grieving at the death of their young mistress. Baron Robert was carefully tended and kept hidden until he was able to be up and about his business.

Florida, 2009

"What a splendid idea!" Amanda MacMurray twirled around so that she could see all of the booth set up on two sides of the fair grounds.

"A middle ages party, and down to the last detail. I can hardly wait for the jousting matches that will be held in the center of the field this afternoon." Her lovely, pale lilac dress brushed the ground as she practically skipped to a food booth. A white lace overskirt and the white lace neckline made a picture worth framing.

Stanley Howzer gazed with love-filled eyes at Amanda. "This will be a great night to announce our engagement at the dinner dance."

She smiled at him and took his arm to walk on to see what the booths offered all around the field.

"Look, Stan. How marvelous. My birthstone. This amethyst and diamond necklace will be just right for my gown. Oh, poo. It costs too much," she pouted as she laid it back on the table.

"Nonsense," Stan answered. He picked up the necklace and, while Amanda wandered on, bartered on a price. He walked behind her and gently placed the necklace around her neck.

"You shouldn't have," she said as she kissed his cheek. "I do love it. The amethyst is my birthstone. Thank you, darling. Oh, thank you so much."

Amanda graciously accepted many compliments on the authenticity of her gown and especially the necklace, at the dance that night.

Anne Carson stopped by the Howzer table with a gasp. "Amanda! Where did you get that absolutely fabulous necklace? It's a match for my earrings. Will you sell it to me?"

"Fraid not," Amanda giggled. "Stan gave this to me as an engagement present. Let me buy your earrings," she grinned.

"I can't do that. These were the last gift that Larry gave me before he died. I'll never part with them."

"I'm sorry," Amanda hugged Anne. "Let's walk around together and let people admire us both."

"Amanda," Stan called, "come here, darling. The photographer wants to take an engagement picture of us for the newspaper."

She happily walked to stand by him and posed as she was requested to stand. Just as the photographer was prepared to snap the picture, they were interrupted by a shrill voice.

"Amanda, wait." Anne rushed up to them. "Wear my earrings for the picture. The complete set will be beautiful on you."

"Thank you, Anne. How sweet of you." Amanda took off her diamond earrings and gave them to Anne to hold. Anne helped Amanda clip the earrings on and stepped back. There was a rushing sound in Amanda's ears, but she smiled for the picture. She felt a little dizzy.

"Now face each other and look lovingly into each other's eyes. I want a romantic shot for your scrapbook," the photographer suggested.

"That won't be hard to do," Amanda smiled and promptly slipped to the floor unconscious.

* * * * *

"Woman! What is the meaning o this? What is yer naime?" A strange man roared at her. Amanda stared at him in dismay.

"Let go of my arm. You're hurting me. Why do you need to know my name? Besides, you didn't introduce yourself, and a gentleman would always introduce himself first."

"Wheest! How verra strange ye talk. If ye e'er a decent woman, ye would have yer maid wee ye."

"Well, listen to you. Talk about strange. My maid," she laughed.

"You're certainly getting into character. Where did everyone go? I don't remember leaving the photographer."

"Woman, ye sound oot o yer moind. What is a phu-phut-arrrgh, whatever ye said?"

"Stop calling me woman. Have you seen Stan Howzer?" *I don't know who this man is but he's sure handsome.* She looked around.

"You dare to talk back to a man, and flip yer skirt like an indecent woman. By the gods, what kind o footwear is that?" He spoke in astonishment as he discovered her lilac sandals with heels.

Amanda grew still and looked at him intently. "Where am I? What happened to the fair grounds? WHO are you?"

"What is a fair ground? So. Ye dint know where ye are. I didna think ye were from here. Ye talk too strange. I'm Baron Robert Rutherford", he bowed, "and yer in Peebles, Scotland."

"No! I couldn't be," Amanda became alarmed. "What year is it?" she asked suspiciously and slowly.

"Woman, are ye mad? It is the year of our Lord, 1498." He suddenly discovered her jewelry. "Where did ye get that?" he yelled growing red in the face.

She looked helplessly at him and then slowly touched her fingers to the necklace. "Stan bought the necklace for me at a booth at the fair grounds for an engagement present, and Anne Carson loaned me her earrings."

"Stan. A booth. Anne's earrings. Ye moost be under a spell. What IS yer name?"

"Why, I'm Amanda MacMurray, and I ----" she screamed in terror as he drew a sword and lunged at her.

"I should a known. I cursed that Ian MacMurray fer cutting o the head o me beautiful woife. He thought he'd left me fer dead. He stole that necklace and those earrings off me woife as she lay in bed after given birth to twin sons, and then he cut off her head." He stopped and struggled to draw a deep breath. "I would love to see a MacMurray dead, but I'll not be as devilish as he was and cut off yer head. Besides, yer too pretty to lose yer head."

Amanda gasped as he grabbed for her. "Coome. Ye moost gae to the castle wee me." He placed strong fingers around her wrist and began dragging her behind him.

Amanda began to scream and pray. "Don't touch me. No! No!"

"Amanda. Amanda, darling. Wake up, please. Shhh. You're safe. Amanda, it's Stan."

She slowly opened her eyes and looked around in wonder. "NOW where am I?"

"You're in the hospital. You fainted while we were having our picture made. Oh, sweetheart, I was so scared. We couldn't wake you up."

"How did I get here?"

"Anne called 911 and an ambulance brought you."

"No," she was upset, "I don't mean that. How did I get **here**?"

Amanda made garbled noises and tried to back up the bed and against the wall.

"Shhh. Easy. It's okay. You're going to be fine," a gentle baritone voice spoke calmly. The voice sounded familiar. She looked up into the face of a young version of Baron Rutherford.

Amanda looked with round, frightened eyes at the doctor taking her pulse. "Who are you?" her voice trembled.

"I'm Doctor Rutherford. Dr. Robert Rutherford."

"Oh," she hesitated, "I must have been dreaming. "I'm so sorry."

"It's alright. I had a hard time getting you to wake up. You were out of it until I took off your jewelry and then you snapped out of it."

"That's it!" Amanda said excitedly as she quickly sat up. "The pieces of jewelry must be worn together for the curse to work."

"Curse?" Stan looked as if he might faint next. Dr. Rutherford gently put his hands on Amanda's shoulders to encourage her to lie down.

She quickly told them of her experience. "I was there most of the afternoon," she finished.

"You were only out about thirty minutes," Stan told her.

"The next time I go back, I'll take a camera and get some pictures to prove where I was, and I'll take pictures and items from here with me to explain where I live," she giggled.

"Oh, no you won't," Anne spoke firmly as she took her earrings off the table. "If the pieces have to be worn together, then you'll not get these again, and I sure have no desire to own the necklace."

"Darling, it was just a dream," Stan patted her hand. "It doesn't mean a thing."

"I'm not so sure," Dr. Rutherford spoke thoughtfully. "I've been tracing my genealogy and I found where one ancestor lost her head during an attack on the family castle. Her husband was badly wounded, but lived. Her twin boys were raised by family servants. One of the twins was my ancestor," he smiled down at Amanda. "Well, one things for sure, old however many greats my granddad was, he was right. You are too beautiful to lose your head." He grinned as he turned to leave the room. "Would you like to go home?"

"Let's get while the getting's good," Stan said as he scooped Amanda up in his arms and almost ran from the room.

Looking over Stan's shoulder, Amanda's eyes found the handsome Dr. Rutherford looking after them. She waggled her fingers of one hand at him, thinking *I'm not through with you, yet -- not through at all.*

THAT'LL LEARN 'IM

"Here we are, darling. The Bay View Real Estate Agency. Are you sure this is what you want, Dan?"

"You betcha. It will put us in a financial squeeze for a short time, but I want you to have the best I can afford."

Daniel Martin looked lovingly at his wife, Cynthia, as he placed an arm around her and urged her to walk in the door ahead of him.

"Good afternoon, how may I help you?" A smiling woman of about fifty greeted them warmly.

"We're Cynthia and Dan Martin and we're interested in property with a nice yard."

"And close to schools, hospitals, churches, shopping and places we might need," Cynthia added with a big smile.

The woman laughed, swinging her shoulder-length, black hair from her face. Her amber eyes sparkled at them as she invited them in. "My name is Allison King. Please have a seat here. I'm sure we have something you'll like." They sat at a round, glass-top table.

"Would you like some ice tea, soft drink or coffee? There's snacks in this basket if you would like something to nibble on. What price range are you considering and do you have a specific location in mind?"

Settled with ice tea and cheese sticks, Dan and Cynthia prepared to look at what the agency had to offer. Allison guessed Dan to be nearing thirty and Cynthia probably middle twenties. She liked their fresh, eager attitude. Smiling to herself, she thought they looked more like brother and sister, both with blonde hair and blue eyes and fair skin.

"I'm a surgeon at Serenity Hospital. It would be great if we could find something near my work. Cynthia is an artist and will need a room with lots of natural light. Of course windows can be added if we find something we like."

"Do you have children?" Allison questioned.

"Half a one," Dan explained with a chuckle as he and Cynthia smiled at each other.

"How wonderful. You're expecting. I take it this is your first one."

"Yes, and we're thrilled. Cynthia has worked hard and helped me finish my medical training. Now I want to give her a nice home where she can do what makes her happy."

"Congratulations. I wish all of the best for you. It's obvious you're very much in love and truly want this baby. I have a good feeling that you're going to be excellent parents. Here, look at these pictures and descriptions of property we have for sale and see if anything catches your attention." She looked at the ringing phone. "Excuse me."

"Good afternoon. Bay View Real Estate. This is Allison King. How may I help you? Well, hi, Gwen." She listened a moment with a smile getting bigger and bigger.

"Gwen, are you positive you want to do this?" Allison listened and then gave a shout of laughter. "You're in luck. A young couple just came in that might be interested. Is it all right if we come over now? Good. Expect us in a few. See you, and thanks a million." Allison hung up chuckling.

"What was that about?" Dan asked curious because they had been mentioned.

"Ask me no questions, et cetera. I feel that you should see this property and hear the owner before I tell you anything about it. I don't want to influence you. Are you free to go look at it now?"

Dan and Cynthia looked at each other and nodded gleefully. Allison guided them through a back door to her station wagon. Fifteen minutes later they drove through an open iron fence on to a circular driveway in front of a house that could only be called a mansion.

A spacious, green lawn stretched all around the house with multi-colored flowers in beds in front on both side of the front steps. Multi-colored impatiens made big circular beds around large trees. Flowering shrubbery formed a barrier in front of an iron fence all the way around the property.

Three half moon concrete steps led to a wide veranda decorated with pots of flowers and potted trees. White wicker furniture was placed in welcoming arrangements. The red brick house boasted floor to ceiling bay windows on either side of the tall, double wide doors.

"Holy catfish," Dan gasped. "I said I wanted to give my wife the best I could afford, but that didn't include the Taj Mahal. I know without asking that I can't afford this."

"Don't be so sure. Come in and talk to Gwen and keep an open mind. You will be surprised," Allison encouraged them.

"I'm surprised I'm here," Cynthia choked. "I've never been in a place like this."

"Come on," Allison urged.

"Hello, everyone."

They looked up to see a beautiful woman, in her middle fifties, at the top of the steps welcoming them with a beaming smile. She was petite, about five-three, maybe one hundred ten pounds. Her curly dark blonde hair was cut so that the end swung in parenthesis around her face. Her bright green eyes were friendly but showed a hint of sadness. "Come on in," she called as if she were inviting them to a game show.

"Whoops." Dan reached to steady Cynthia as she stumbled on a step while trying to see everything. "Easy, honey. It's okay."

"Dan, I feel so out of place here."

"We're just looking, darling. Keep in mind that you might get some decorating ideas, and, who knows, I might be able to afford something like this in the future."

"Dan, I don't care if it's a log cabin. I'll be happy being your wife and the mother of our babies."

"That's wonderfully sweet," Gwen sighed. "There was a time when I had stars in my eyes like that, but now --" She turned a welcoming grin at them. "I'm Gwen Ziegler. Let me show you around. Would you like something cold to drink first?"

"No, thank you," Cynthia answered looking around with wide eyes. She drew a deep breath as they stepped through the front door. "Oh, my. Marble floors and big vertical mirrors on the walls in the foyer. Cream-colored, plush carpets all over the place. This certainly wasn't decorated with the idea of having children. Oh," she gasped, "I'm sorry. I have a bad habit of thinking aloud, especially when

I'm nervous, and I'm sure nervous to find myself in a palatial place like this. In fact I ___ Stop me, Dan."

"Don't apologize. You're right about the children. My husband, Marcus, made the decision that we would not have a family until he was well established in his work as a financial advisor and broker. He's eleven years older than I and I did worry about waiting too long. I wanted children desperately. The years flew by and the time never seemed right --- at least for him."

"Are you moving?" Dan broke in. "Forgive me. I'm curious as to why you're selling such a beautiful home. It's obvious a lot of time, thought and love has gone into furnishing and decorating."

"I'll tell you all about it in a few minutes. Let me show you through the house. Let's go first through the living room, then through the atrium to the loggia."

They walked through a gorgeous room with loads of windows. The room was almost filled with potted plants and potted trees. Passing through they walked out on a mosaic tiled area leading to a large oval-shaped swimming pool.

"Now I know I'm dreaming," Cynthia remarked uneasily.

"Honey, that atrium would be a wonderful place for an art studio for you. The large area in the corner could be fenced in to make a play area for the babies," Dan smiled.

"Don't hurry to make a decision yet," Gwen chuckled. "Allow me to tell you the circumstances of my selling before you decide. You'll be pleasantly surprised."

They walked upstairs through five bedrooms, each with a huge cedar-lined walk-in closet and a full bath. They had seen a half bath off the foyer and a bath beside the kitchen.

"This is what I've dreamed of owning," Dan gazed around with sparkling eyes and spoke wistfully. "It feels like a happy place.

"Yes, and that lovely big back yard with humongous maple trees. What a fabulous place for children and a dog. A couple of dogs and a kitten. And a wonderful place for you to entertain," Cynthia smiled as she had her own daydream.

"Gwen, why don't you tell them the good news now," Allison said.

Gwen looked at Dan and Cynthia and smiled. "Let's sit here. Cynthia, Dan, I've watched you two and listened to your conversation. It's obvious you're truly in love and honestly are looking forward to having children. I want to help. Consider me your god fairy," she laughed.

"Help us? How?" Dan asked startled. "We're strangers to you and you sure don't owe us anything."

"A stranger is a friend you've yet to meet," Gwen interjected and smiled sardonically. "I'm a private person, but I want to share some very personal things with you. First, I want to say, I'm envious of you."

"Envious?" Cynthia repeated puzzled.

"Yes. You see, when Marcus and I married nineteen years ago, I worked to help him further his education -- just as you helped Dan. When he opened his office, I gave up my job as a registered nurse, which I loved, to help him socially. He felt he had to entertain a lot to get clients. I ached for children, but Marcus kept putting it off. Finally I realized we would not be having children, but I loved my husband so much that I didn't allow it to upset me." She hesitated to wipe her eyes and take a long drink of ice tea.

"To make a long, and boring, story short, two weeks ago I was helping Marcus pack for one of his many business trips. I found two airline tickets to Aruba and was excited thinking he intended to surprise me. I hurried to the hair dressers and ran needed errands. When I returned home, Marcus was gone, but he had left a typed letter on the dresser. It was plain to see the letter had been typed at his office some time before that day."

"Oh, my goodness," Cynthia interrupted. "Are you sure you want to share this with us."

"I'm sure. I need to explain why I'm selling. The letter stated that he felt I was holding him back. He was taking his twenty-eight year old secretary with him for an indefinite time. Incidentally, she's pregnant. He had applied for a divorce and I would be hearing from his attorney soon. He planned to marry his secretary, however, she doesn't want to live in a house I've lived in, therefore, I'm to sell everything, liquidate all stocks and bonds and we would split everything fifty-fifty. He said he wanted to be fair to me." Gwen gave a choked laugh. "He said he knows how fair I am and he trusts me to handle everything." They could see she had cried in the past and still felt a little raw about the dirty deal she had gotten.

Allison was laughing until tears were streaming down her cheeks. Dan and Cynthia looked at each other in bewilderment.

Gwen continued. "I don't care about the money. I have a substantial inheritance from my grandparents which I've never touched and it's been gaining interest. Further more, I'm anxious to go back to nursing." She stopped and leaned closer to the young couple. "Meeting you two, I've decided to price the house at -- shall we say -- fifty thousand."

"Fifty thousand dollars?" Dan and Cynthia yelled at the same time.

"If you think that's too much we'll discuss price."

"What do houses in this area sell for?" Dan asked Allison.

"Anywhere from three quarters of a million to a million and a half."

"And you would take fifty thousand from us?' Dan spluttered.

"Sure. That's twenty-five thousand for Marcus' share, less expenses of course. By the way, there a two year old Cadillac in the garage you can have for -- oh a hundred. Marcus said he knew he could trust me because I've always been honest with him," she chuckled.

"Can we pay insurance premiums and taxes on property this size? Cynthia asked anxiously. Then it hit her. "One hundred dollars for a two year old Cadillac!"

"Sure thing. Remember, I'm splitting fifty-fifty."

"Would we run into trouble from any source because of the price?" Dan asked hesitantly. It was obvious he was interested, but he was fearful because of the circumstances.

"No. Marcus left power of attorney with his attorney. I happen to know things on his attorney that he would not want his wife's family to find out. Sneaky and dirty of me, but it's my way of getting revenge. Beats going to prison for murder." she laughed. "His attorney will sign any documents that I might require. He'd better if he knows what's good for him."

"Can we afford to maintain it?" Cynthia asked hopefully.

"Did I mention that the majority of the furniture will go with the house?"

Gwen grinned.

Dan and Cynthia gasped and hugged each other like two children afraid and seeking reassurance. Cynthia tried to speak but only squeaked. She then sat speechless.

"Let us talk it over and get back to you," Dan said lamely, getting up to pace.

After a moment of silence, Cynthia reached and touched his arm. "Darling, I know you're going to have a successful practice. I have a feeling we can swing it. Besides if we can't maintain it, think of the profit we'll make if we have to sell. As long as we're together we'll conquer anything."

Dan drew a deep breath. "Okay," whatever you say. He sat down looking as if he were too shaky to stand.

"Hurrah!" Gwen cheered.

"Gwen is like a sister to me and my best friend. I'll help in any way that I can." Allison leaned back in her chair laughing loudly. "Oh, Marcus. That'll learn 'em, dern 'im." she whooped

CUT OFF YOUR NOSE

Her gasp of surprise, and a quick jerk to the newspaper caused coffee to slosh out and burn her hand. Hearing her yelp of pain, Dexter, her cat gave a yowl of irritation and jumped from her lap to hide under the table.

Marilyn Baker pushed her breakfast dishes aside so that she had room to open the paper fully and read the article. "That's the cute little girl I saw yesterday," she told Dexter excitedly.

Quickly she perused the article telling of the kidnapping of the three year old daughter of a wealthy judge. A picture showed a tearful woman, in charge of the day school stating, "The two men showed me IDs and I really thought they were the chauffer and bodyguard sent for Lynette. I even called the number they gave me and a woman identified them over the phone. Oh, that dear, sweet child. How could anyone be so cruel to an innocent child?"

The police explained to her that the woman who identified them over the phone was part of the group who had taken the child. "These people commonly have someone call a number and a confederate is at the phone ready to cover and lie for them."

"Dexter, I was sitting on a park bench across the street from where the men had parked the limousine. Remember, I told you I had done some colored pencil sketches of the school and the cherry blossoms. As the men put the little girl in the car I heard her say, "Are we really going to see my daddy?" One of the men glared angrily at me. I just smiled and went on sketching. I sure hope the police have a lot of clues."

Marilyn hugged Dexter and kissed him on his nose. "Be a good boy. I have to go to the Bide-A-Wee baby shop. They've hired me to do some sketches for a new advertisement for the store." She cleaned the kitchen, cleaned the litter box, and put down fresh water for her cat. Waving at the sleeping cat, she left the apartment, carefully locked the door and walked out.

Marilyn walked the four city blocks to the store and was soon engrossed in planning the ad campaign with the store manager. Leaving there, she went to an art supply store to purchase some items she needed for the next job. After a quick lunch she went to the Hug-A-Bug pet store to discuss her ideas for a new promotion for them.

As she left the store she met a friend who was a legal secretary at the county courthouse. "Hi, Marilyn. I'm so glad I ran into you. Do you have time to grab a cup of coffee and chat a while?"

"Hey, Joan. Sure. I'd love to visit with you."

The two young women walked a few doors down to the Fill-er-Up Sandwich Shop. Marilyn ordered apple pie and coffee and Joan ordered Banana Cream pie and coffee.

Joan was not her usual bubbly self. Marilyn looked at her friend concerned. "Is there something wrong, Joan?"

"Didn't you read the paper this morning or hear the news?"

"Yes, but what in particular are you talking about?"

"Judge Bill Conroy is a widower who is raising his baby girl with the help of a housekeeper. He recently decided that the little girl needed friends her own age and enrolled her in a pre kindergarten day school. Yesterday she was taken from the school by two strange men. He lost his wife to cancer when the baby was ten months old. Now she's in danger. He's beside himself, and blaming himself."

"I can well imagine how frightened, and angry, he must be. Do the police know why the men took the judge's child?"

"Yes. This morning he had a call. A distorted voice demanded that he release the mob boss, Antonio Petrulucci, or he would never see his little girl again. Petrulucci is serving a forty year sentence in the state prison."

"That's horrible. He can't, in good conscience, release such a dangerous criminal, but, on the other hand, he can't take chances with his daughter's life. Did they say they would kill the child?"

"No. The poor baby must be so frightened and confused. The person did say he would never see his daughter again. That could mean a lot of things."

"You're right. Gee, I wish I could help." With a deep sigh, Marilyn stood. "I hate to run, but I have work to do. I'm glad I got to see you, Joan. We must get together soon. It's been too long."

"Are you leaving me here alone so soon?"

"I must. I have a lot of orders for drawings and I need to work while the natural light is still good. One of the drawings is an oil painting for the new library. Take care. Ta tah."

The two young women hugged and parted. Marilyn walked light-heartedly up the outside steps to her apartment building. She used a key to open the outer door and then walked down the hall to her first-floor apartment overlooking the beautiful flower gardens.

I locked this door this morning. I know I did she thought as she cautiously pushed her open apartment door. Her heart leaped as she noticed the ripped couch cushions, overturned potted plants and general destruction in the living room/ dining room area. "Dexter," she called fearfully. "Oh, Dexter, please be here. Be hiding somewhere." A search didn't reveal the cherished cat.

Marilyn ran to the manager's apartment and feverishly rang the bell. As Mr. Hurley opened his door, she spouted. "I just got home. I did lock my door this morning. It's open. My apartment is vandalized, and messed up and my cat is gone. A window at the back is open, but Dexter's gone," she finished on a sob.

"Calm down, Miss Baker. I think I know what you're saying. Let me call the police and you stay here with me until they come. They won't like it if you destroy evidence."

"I didn't destroy anything. Someone destroyed my things, and I can't find my cat," she was almost yelling. "How did they get in?"

"I hear you. Come in and sit down. I don't know yet how they entered the building or your apartment." He gently led her into his front room and seated her on a couch. He then called the police and told them what Marilyn had reported to him.

The police were there in a few minutes. They wouldn't allow anyone into Marilyn's apartment until they had completed their investigation. After about half an hour one of the police came to get Marilyn. The manager went with her.

"Why?" she wailed. "Why would anyone do this to me? I don't know of a soul that would be this angry at me. Where is my cat? He's been neutered and declawed. He can't survive long on his own outside."

"Is this who you're looking for?" A police came grinning to Marilyn holding a very contented Dexter.

"Dexter! Oh, my baby. Where did you go? Where did you find him?"

"He was sitting in the open window. Apparently he had been out in the flowers. We've had a nice conversation, but he didn't give me any helpful information."

"Thank you," she hugged Dexter to her. "I was so afraid for him. Have you found any clues as to who did this and why?"

"Not exactly, ma'am. The pillows were slashed with something sharp and the plants were just turned over. We think this was done to hide the real reason for them being here. If we knew what they were after, it would be a clue as to who they were. Come into the room where you have your art supplies."

All of them trooped into the guest bedroom that Marilyn used for storage and for art material. "Oh, my word!" she whispered. Paint was slung all over the room, a drawing on an eased was cut and ripped and brushes were slung all over the floor.

The officer in charge let her look for a minute and then spoke to her. "Can you find anything specific missing?"

"No," she said softly and slowly as she looked around the apartment. Walking around the art room she suddenly stopped. "My sketch books. They're gone. Why would anyone want them? They're just large books of blank paper that I keep my ideas in until I'm ready to work on them."

"Are you afraid to stay here alone, or do you know someone you can call to stay with you? The office inquired kindly.

Mr. Hurley stepped back into the room. "I've sent for two men who help me in emergencies. We'll clean the apartment for her." He turned to Marilyn. "Wouldn't you like to go to a friend's place for the night, at least until we can get this place cleaned and a new lock on the door?"

"I guess so," she answered hesitantly. "Let me pack a bag and get supplies for Dexter." She called Joan and, after Marilyn told her story, Joan insisted that she and Dexter come to her apartment.

Two hours later, sitting up in bed, Marilyn and Joan were talking. Marilyn got her folder and pulled out a sketch pad. "This one I've been working in this week is the only one I have left."

"Maybe if you work a while you'll feel better and can get to sleep," Joan told her gently.

"Joan, I keep thinking of the men who took the judge's daughter. I can remember one of them who stared straight at me "

"Why don't you draw him? The police would appreciate the help. If they recognize him, it might help them find Lynette."

The next morning Joan called the courthouse and explained why she would not be in to work. The police had suggested that she stay with Marilyn for the time being.

Marilyn picked up her colored pencils and positioned the sketch pad ready for work. "Oh, Joan, I know I can help but it will mean everyone will know who I really am."

"So what. You're Princess Magrita Adubah of Monclosa. You'll be admired because you wanted to succeed in your art work on your merit alone instead of your royal connections."

"But I'm here under an assumed name."

"You said it was your mother's name before she married your father. There's no law, that I know of, in using your mother's name."

"If you say so," she sighed and began to work.

"Whooo," Joan shuddered. "That's a mean looking man. I bet the police will have an idea who he is. Joan called and asked for the officer assigned to the judge's case. She briefly told him why she wanted him to come to her apartment.

The police came to Joan's apartment in about ten minutes. Marilyn explained, "I remember one of the men that I saw with the little girl. Maybe you can recognize him, or someone at the station might know him."

"Hey, lady. You've done a super job. This is Victor Stalvey. He's one of Antonio Petrulucci's hatchet men. Boy, is the Captain going to be pleased with you."

Marilyn stood up excitedly. "That's why they stole my sketch books. They saw me drawing and didn't know what I was doing. I bet they thought I had already drawn pictures of them. Well, their little deed boomeranged. If they had not broken in, I might not have thought of drawing his picture. They did themselves dirt. As the old saying goes, they cut off their own nose to spite their face."

The officers called their Captain and he joined them in Joan's apartment. He gave orders for Victor, and anyone with him, to be picked up.

That afternoon Marilyn and Joan joined Judge Conley at the police station while Marilyn looked at mug shots. "That's one for sure," she said pointing to Victor's picture. "And this might be the other one."

"He's one of Petrulucci's men, too. His name is Shelley D'Orcea. Pick both of them up," the Captain ordered. He turned to the group. "Where you see one, you usually see the other. We've got them this time. If I find Petrulucci gave orders to his men to kidnap the little girl, we'll add another twenty years to his sentence. He and his men can serve time together."

Later the Judge and the Captain were talking to Petrulucci. "You've done it to yourself," Judge Conley told him. "You've added another twenty years to your sentence by orchestrating the kidnapping of my daughter, and if she's been harmed in any way, I'm going to jack up the jail and throw you under it and lower it. You're going to be buried for life."

After Victor and Shelley had been arrested, Victor's sister confessed that they brought the little girl to her. "They told me the child belonged to one of their buddies; that his wife had died and he couldn't take care of the little girl now. I went out of town for three days to visit some relatives and took her with me. That's why I missed the news. I would never have agreed to be a part in such a horrendous act."

The Judge hugged his daughter and thanked Marilyn over and over. "Is there something I can do for you since you refuse to take a reward?" He looked at her appreciatively.

"No. Thank you. My reward is knowing that this precious child is back with her daddy."

"I know what she needs," Lynette said looking impishly up at her daddy.

"What's that, Munchkin?" the proud father asked.

"We need ice cream," she answered with a big grin.

"Works for me," the Judge laughed. "How about you, Marilyn?"

Joan nudged her from behind and winked at her. Joan started walking away. "I need to go by my office and check on some papers. I'll see you later."

They didn't see Joan dash into a restroom and peer out a crack in the door. She smiled with satisfaction as she saw the three of them coming down the hall. Lynette walked between her father and Marilyn with each adult holding one of her little hands.

As they passed the restroom, Lynette clearly said, "I'm so happy, I want to skip."

"Me, too," her daddy said with a laugh.

Joan saw the Captain and several officers grinning at the trio as they went skipping down the hall and out the door. Joan sighed happily. "And they lived happily ever after," she whispered.

SURPRISE! SURPRISE!

Classical music drifted softly over the well-kept lawn to the gazebo. A heavy, sweet smell of roses, jasmine and gardenia floated on the air. The early summer was great in Zephyrhills, Florida because the city had something for everyone of all ages.

Sulyn gave a deep sigh of contentment as she closed her eyes and listened to the string quartet practicing. The next day her parents were celebrating their twenty-ninth wedding anniversary and her graduation from law school.

Sweet memories filtered her sleepy mind as she remembered idyllic days growing up here on Paradise Acres, her parents' estate.

"Ssst."

Sulyn's eyes flew open although she sat still. *What in the world was that? I hope it wasn't a snake.*

"I thought you'd never get here," a man's angry voice hissed,

"Keep your shirt on, love. I had to finish my work before I could leave."

"Yeah. Well, little girl, you'd better have good news for me."

"Let's walk down through the flower gardens and I'll tell you all the news. And it is good.

Sulyn tried unsuccessfully to see through the tangle of vines and flowers around the gazebo, but couldn't see clearly. She had enjoyed the privacy the vegetation gave in the gazebo, but now was frustrated by it. *Who are they? Oh, well, it doesn't make any difference. They're probably some of the temporary people that were hired to help with the preparations for the party. They're probably on a romantic tryst.* She smiled to herself.

"Sulyn. Darling, where are you?"

"I'm here, mother. In the gazebo."

"Please come to the house. I need your in-put to help me make a decision."

Sulyn quickly left the gazebo and walked across the wide, beautifully landscaped lawn, looking over her shoulder to see if she could identify the couple. No luck.

As she crossed the veranda and through the front door, her mother was frowning at tall flowers in taller, white wicker baskets. She was walking from one side of the foyer to the other, talking to herself as she moved.

"Oh, there you are. Honey, do you think these baskets will look better here at the foot of the stairs, or should I place them, just inside, on either side of the front door?"

They both looked up the five feet wide beautifully varnished red cherry stairs with a plush gold carpet runner. After placing the tall baskets in both locations, they agreed that the foot of the stairs would be the best location.

A young woman walked out of the kitchen, through the large dining room and to the vestibule where Sulyn and Mrs. Cantrell stood. She was carrying small freshly-washed crystal bowls that would hold nuts and various snacks.

"Sulyn, this is Anne Boyd. She has been kind enough to help us out temporarily. Her sister and cousin will be here for the next two days to help with the party and to clean up afterwards."

"Hello Anne. I'm glad you could spar the time to make it easier for mother."

"It's my pleasure. I need the money so that I can continue my education, and it's a joy to work in a beautiful home with such lovely people."

"The man working outside in the flower beds," Mrs. Cantrell continued, "is Jim Baker. He has done a beautiful job with the flower beds and lawn. He pulled a ton of weeds, planted additional flowers and fertilized the lawn."

Anne went on about her business while Sulyn and her mother studied the list of things to do.

The day of the party dawned bright and clear. A soft, gentle rain had fallen during the night making the air fresh and clean. The grass looked as if it had been freshly washed and rolled out. As the sun came up, the moisture, clinging to everything, evaporated and everything was just right.

By noon everything was prepared and in place. The Best Bites Caterers had all the food brought in and the extra people, hired to help serve the one hundred plus guests, had arrived on time. The young college men who were to park cars were dressed and in place ready to help the guests. Long tables with snow-white cloths were set up under the big trees to serve the guests at a sit-down dinner.

Mrs. Cantrell called to all the people working to get a plate and eat. "I don't want any of you passing out from hunger when there's so much food here," she laughed.

Mr. Cantrell, much to everyone's relief, had arrived that morning from an out-of-town business trip. He hurriedly showered and dressed.

Around two o'clock, Mrs. Cantrell went to the pantry and slid open a secret door to a closet. Her screams brought everyone running. Mr. Cantrell and Sulyn elbowed their way through. Sulyn gasped. Mr. Cantrell said some choice, shocked words.

Their butler was lying in the closet with a bleeding head wound. "Is he -" Mrs. Cantrell asked weakly. Sulyn quickly knelt by him and placed two fingers on the carotid artery in his throat.

"No. He's alive, but his pulse is thready." She looked up at one of the college boys. "Paul, call 911 and ask for an ambulance and the police."

"It's gone," Mrs. Cantrell gasped through sobs.

"What?" Mr. Cantrell asked loudly. "What's gone?"

"Grandmother's sterling silver tableware. I had it delivered from the bank vault yesterday afternoon. I didn't tell a soul because I wanted it to be a surprise. It was to be a graduation present for Sulyn. Complete service for one hundred twenty-five people. Almost four thousand dollars." She was crying so hard they could barely understand her.

"Now, now, sweetheart." Mr. Cantrell was angry and upset, but he put his arms around his wife to console her. "Just calm down. We'll figure all this out. Who knew the silverware was there?"

"I told you, no one," she answered shakily and sharply.

"Someone knew, or Reginald wouldn't be lying there with a head wound and the silverware wouldn't be gone," Mr. Cantrell spoke thoughtfully.

"Well, I sure don't know anything about any of this," Anne Boyd declared. "I have only been here for two days and I didn't even know that secret place was there," she went on nervously. "And I sure didn't hear you call and ask for it to be delivered."

Everyone milled around nervously while the EMTs took Reginald out on a gurney to take him to the hospital. "He's sure a lucky man. Most head wounds like that send the person into a coma and they never wake up," one medic remarked.

The workers talked softly and excitedly among themselves.

"Whoa. Hold it right there," Sulyn spoke with authority. Anne, how did you know mother called and asked for the silver to be delivered? For all you know, she could have gone to the bank and picked it up."

"Well, uh," Anne stuttered, "I just guessed, or maybe she did say something."

"Did you call the bank, sweetheart?" Mr. Cantrell frowned.

"Why, yes," Mrs. Cantrell answered. "I had been to the bank last week and told Hershel that I would need it delivered by special messenger. He said just to let him know, so I called and told him it was time."

"How long have you and Jim Baker been going together?" Sulyn snapped at Anne.

"Uh, umm, not long," she said with a slight stutter.

"Ha! That's it, dad. Mother, remember when you called to me yesterday and I answered that I was in the gazebo?"

"Yes, darling."

"While I was sitting there, I heard a couple talking about good news. The man told the woman that she had better have good news for him. I now recognize Anne's voice and I bet the man was Jim Baker. It's obvious the news Anne had for him was about the silver being delivered."

Mrs. Cantrell delicately blew her nose and wiped her eyes. "I remember now." She drew her five-four up straight and looked straight at Anne. "Jim was in the kitchen lifting the heavy boxes of punch bowls and cups. He helped bring in the four boxes of silver from the messenger's truck. I told him to sit them on the table. Later I had Reginald put them in the pantry. Jim must have sneaked around to watch where I placed the silver. I bet he came back later and Reginald caught him stealing the items. He probably thought he had killed Reginald so he wouldn't tell who had hit him. Anne must have been in on it."

"No! I won't take the blame alone," Anne declared.

"Sulyn, call the police back," Mr. Cantrell spoke angrily. "I want Anne arrested and the police can put out an APB on Jim. He's long gone."

"Please wait," Anne begged. "If I tell you what you want to know, will you let me go?"

"Anne, a crime has been committed, a serious one," Mr. Cantrell explained. "It will be a lot easier for you if you'll just tell the truth."

The police walked in with early arriving guests.

"Well," Anne began, "I grew up real poor and didn't have much. Jim convinced me that if I'd help him, we could get married and go away from here. I'd hardly been out of the county," Anne sobbed.

Sulyn, I'm proud of you and I know mother is, too. We certainly didn't waste money sending you to law school," her dad chuckled. "Or maybe, after today, you'd rather be a detective.

"Dad, remember the secret I said I'd tell you when I got home?" Sulyn grinned.

"What!?" screamed Mr. Cantrell.

"Just kidding, dad. Just kidding. Don't have a stroke. Maybe I'll be an investigating attorney like Perry Mason or Ben Matlock. If you'll look out the window, you'll see the secret I had for you."

The police started out the door with Anne in handcuffs. "Hey! Look at those guys," one officer stated. "They look like they might belong to the Mafia."

Sulyn stifled a laugh. "Gracious. Don't let them hear you say that. They are bodyguards for that man over there."

The second policeman gave a startled exclamation. "Is that who I think it is? That looks like ---"

"Governor Lawton Chiles," Mr. Cantrell spoke surprised. "Who invited him? Oh, I didn't mean that the way it sounded. I'm thrilled. We used to golf together." He hurried over to welcome his old friend.

"How wonderful," Mrs. Cantrell hugged Sulyn. "Honey, you couldn't have given us a nicer surprise for our anniversary."

The party was a huge success. No fancy tableware, but the guests understood and enjoyed themselves immensely.

Jim Baker was found a week later with the pawn tickets for the silver and other items he had stolen. He was given twelve years in prison for theft and attempted murder. Anne was sentenced to three years for being his accomplice.

Sulyn went to visit Anne in jail. Her compassionate heart was burdened on behalf of Anne. She knew Anne had trusted the wrong person and had learned a valuable lesson.

"Sulyn, I'm so ashamed. I didn't know until the trial that Jim never intended to take me with him."

"I know. I'm sorry, too, but you've learned a valuable lesson. We need to be satisfied with what we have and where we are. We need to work hard to earn what we want and then know how to take care of it legally.

Sulyn has opened a successful law practice. She has several people working with her; two of them are excellent detectives. People have learned that she is honest and will stand by her clients. She represents some that can't afford to pay her.

Mr. and Mrs. Cantrell took a long cruise on the Mediterranean soon after their party. Mrs. Cantrell was so happy to get her Grandmother's silver back so that she could give it to Sulyn to start building her hope chest.

Oh, yes. Governor Chiles said he didn't know when he had enjoyed a party as much as the one at the Cantrell's. After he heard about the near disasters that morning, he told Sulyn he would love to have her on his staff.

She thanked him and told him that she needed to be on her own and do what she could for her community.

I Prayed -- And the Devil Answered

This is the absolute truth as it happened to me. It isn't a matter of life and death, but the death of trust in certain people.

Satan is not always as obvious as people might think, and he does trick even Christians. He also uses weak Christians to do his work.

I prayed for financial guidance and in two days had a response which seemed to be an answer to prayer. Much later, I reasoned that Satan had answered. The devastating part was that Satan had used a deacon from a church to do his dirty work.

My prayer was for divine guidance to show me how to invest a modest sum of money so that I could have a decent return. A worry to all of us, as we get older, is that we might lose our independence and be dependant upon others. A widow, with a small income, I was no exception. I'm not then, and never have been, greedy for a lot of money; I just don't want to be a burden on my daughter.

A neighbor, and a close friend, came to my house telling me that he and his wife knew a deacon in their church, in another city, who had invented a microscopic disc to be used as a security alarm. He said that a world renowned hotel chain was interested in purchasing this disc, but the deacon needed financial backing to get it on the market. If we would invest five thousand dollars for a share, we would be assured of at least a fifty thousand dollar return in about eight months.

I told my neighbor of my prayer and we were sure this was an answer. I ask to meet the deacon and question him. A few days later, the couple brought this man to my house. I told him of my prayer and he said, "Praise the Lord. This is Heaven's answer." He seemed to understand my situation and continued to assure us that we would have a good return. He stated that, when the sale of the disc was completed, we would each earn at least eighty thousand dollars. (Remember the old saying, 'if it seems too good to be true, it is?') I asked him what would happen to our investment if the deal fell through. He stated that he would return our investment from his own pocket.

"You will be the seventeenth and eighteenth stockholders, which is all I want. I also want only practicing Christians involved and a promise that you'll support missionaries." He was confident that we would all be satisfied. We sang some gospel choruses and stood in a circle to have prayer. I was uneasy but the three of them talked me into it.

I went to my bank the next day and borrowed the money on an equity loan using my house as collateral. I didn't tell my daughter because I wanted to surprise her. Believe me, after the disastrous experience I had, I discuss everything with her now.

Three months went by and we had heard nothing. I called the deacon and ask for some proof of investment. He said our cancelled checks were sufficient. "They have offered me sixty million. I will keep fifty-one percent and the rest will be divided among all of you."

It was exciting. The deacon called us often and, when at church, told my neighbors of a bright future. Time crawled by and he told us that the hotel chain wanted their Chief of Security to try the device in their hotels in Miami. It would be a few more months before the deal was complete.

Six months and still we heard nothing. I called him and he said they were taking the disc overseas to determine how it would work anywhere in the world. He also said they had dropped their offer to forty million. Still not bad.

I ask him for proof of our owning stock and he sent us a certificate with the cooperate name, my name, statement of my owning one share and signed by him and another person. I thought it was strange that there was no notary stamp or a state of Florida seal. Stupid me. I was too trusting.

I called him again and ask what would happen if someone else took his idea and stole it and we were left out. He said he had taken out a sixty-eight million dollar insurance policy on the deal.

Thirteen months later we received a copy of a letter on the official stationary of the hotel. Three vice-presidents of the hotel had met with the deacon and his attorney to finalize the deal. They had signed a statement. There was also a letter enclosed from a prominent local attorney stating that he was handling the deal and all was well. I called the deacon and said I was going to talk to the attorney. He told me not to because it might harm the deal since it was almost complete.

A couple of weeks later, my neighbors came to tell me that the deacon, and his wife, had met them at church with hugs and beaming faces to say that the deal with the hotel chain had fallen through, however, a well-known towel company was going to pick up the deal.

Two months more and no word. I called the deacon and he coldly told me that he was doing the best he could with the towel company. He also raved about us being so greedy and said that some stockholders were complaining about the offered price. I comforted him and said that twenty million was still a lot to share among eighteen stockholders. There was a quiet moment and he mumbled that there were actually sixty-six stockholders. I was too stunned to ask the questions that I should have as he quickly hung up.

The next month I called and his wife bawled me out for bothering them. Nineteen months after the first contact, and a few days before Christmas, the deacon called us and left a message on the answering machine. He was singing, "Hallelujah, thine the glory." He said he had just come from his attorney's office and had seen the checks being printed. This was Thursday and he said the checks would reach us the following Monday by registered mail. We eagerly waited. A week went by. Nothing.

At the end of the week I called his house. His daughter answered and started screaming at me. She said her daddy had more to lose than any of us and we were making her mother sick by calling. I apologized. Little did I know the heartache that was in that house on that day.

Another deacon, who had invested also, called my neighbors and said when the man's family got up that morning they found his driver's license, credit cards, keys and everything on the dresser, but no sign of him. The family thought he had gone off to commit suicide. He said there had never been a disc, or a company. The deacon had taken over two million dollars from many people and not just in the state of Florida. I was appalled to learn that attorneys, one judge and several prominent business men had invested with him. It didn't make me feel any better.

Dozens of us reported to the police who investigated and turned it over to the state's attorney. The deacon had lied, stolen, cheated and manipulated people for over two years. Yet, some of the people in his church were sorry for him and were trying to cover up for him.

He had stolen the stationary from the hotel and from the attorney's office. He had written the letters and forged the signatures. I could not get over how bold he had been in his criminal activities. He had fooled people who worked in the law and got away with it for that length of time.

Why hadn't his family been suspicious? Did they know of his duplicity? How could they accept that a vacuuming cleaner salesman could afford a forty thousand dollar wedding for his daughter, bought a truck and a delivery truck and set his son up in business and bought many expensive items for the house? They took, but why weren't they questioning him. My feelings were that they should be required to repay us. The court didn't agree with me. I felt as if I had lost double the amount since I gave it to him and no longer had it and had to repay the loan with interest.

It is sad to know that Satan works through people whom we perceive to be Christians. This has not shattered my faith. I still believe in prayer and Divine guidance. I suspect that Satan is pleased to have caused so much pain and loss.

After several months the man was found, arrested and stood trial. The judge gave him five years in prison with fifteen years probation. During the fifteen years he was to work and pay all of us back. If not, he would serve the entire twenty years in jail. He only served nine months, left the area, and I heard later he had a job in an automobile salesroom. We'll never see our money.

Twelve years have passed since that time. I'm sure that Satan's intention was to weaken the name of Christianity. It only made me stronger. I still trust, maybe too much, but I do question a lot before I get involved in anything. I can still sing, "My God is real, for I can feel Him in my soul."

DARK SECRET

June 14

The Yacht Club of Lincoln, Oregon rang with laughter and festival ecstasy as the elite of the area celebrated nineteen year old Phoenix Kennedy's acceptance into pre-law school, and his grandmother's, Pamela Kennedy, sixty-fifth birthday.

Ardent emotions ran high as the invited guests expected Phoenix's uncle, Judge Montel Kennedy, to announce his engagement to a well-known, and much loved attorney, Izabella Izaturbi. Her intelligence and sweet personality were excelled only by her ability to win cases with a compassionate heart.

Montel's wife, Alesandra, whom he adored, had been killed in a fall from the balcony from the ninth floor apartment where they lived at the time. It was eighteen years and seven months ago to the day of this party. Everyone loved Montel and had loved Alesandra. They had grieved with him through the years and had decided that he would never remarry. Now they were delighted that he had found someone with whom he could be happy.

Montel, at the time of his wife's death, was a leading defense attorney. If it had not been for his brother, Cole, and Cole's wife, Monica, Montel would have given up and become a bum. At least a recluse. Montel and Alesandra had looked forward to having children. The day she had informed him that she was six weeks pregnant, they were too happy to describe and had invited his family to celebrate with them at a dinner theatre. After five years of marriage they were finally going to have their heart's desire.

Montel had been called from the dinner by a wealthy television celebrity who had been in the news and accused of a charge that Montel believed him to be innocent of. No one had shown up at the office and, a little after eleven o'clock, he had decided to go home. His taxi pulled around the corner facing the apartment building where he lived. He was astonished to see police cars, ambulance and people milling around like ants in a disturbed nest.

Not only was his beautiful, beloved, pregnant wife lying dead on the sidewalk, but later no one would admit calling him to his office. Cole and Monica were kneeling by the body and grieving inconsolably. At first Montel didn't register that they were by the body of his wife. When he recognized, and fell to his knees beside her body. He was too upset to ask them how they happened to be there. He had left them at the dinner theatre to take his mother home and he had brought Alesandra home and left her before going to his office.

After his wife's funeral, Montel had refused to leave the apartment for days. He wasn't eating, couldn't sleep, hadn't shaved or bathed or cared how he looked. Cole and Monica had finally visited and demanded that he go on a cruise with them and get away from the area for a while. He acquiesced and found that he relaxed more than he thought he would. He even enjoyed the evening shows and dancing with Monica. He was delighted with them when they told him they were expecting their first child.

After returning home, he gradually began working again. In three years he had been offered a judgeship and he had accepted. He buried himself in his work.

Monica and Cole had a son whom they named Phoenix. He became the apple of his uncle's eye. No one but Montel thought it was unusual that Cole and Monica both had blue eyes, but their son had violet eyes -- just as Alesandra had.

The residents of Lincoln City, and the county, admired Judge Kennedy for his unbiased decisions and his deep concern for children and single mothers. There were always a few who felt they had received a raw deal, not admitting that they had been caught in a crime. Now everyone was delighted that Montel had met Izabella and dated her frequently. After all, it had been slightly over eighteen years since Alesandra's death. The party guests were thrilled expecting to hear him announce his engagement to the beautiful, intelligent Izabella.

Shouts of joy and encouragement went up as hundreds of balloons were released from the ceiling and Pamela was encouraged to blow out the candle on her cake. Glasses were raised in several toasts. Everyone waited with expectant smiles when Phoenix stood and raised his glass. The room became quiet. He looked around the crowded room with a solemn expression and looked at his Uncle Montel who smiled at him. Pamela, his Grandmother, waited with a big smile expecting to hear him say something wonderful about her.

Phoenix turned to face his Grandmother, raised his glass higher, hesitated and smashed it to the floor. There was a gasp from the crowd and then silence as they strained to listen. "What I'm going to say," he told the perplexed family and guests, "will sound as if I'm losing my mind. With God as my witness, I'm telling the complete truth, but I can't explain it. Eighteen years and seven months ago, on this very date, Grandmother, you killed my mother who was pregnant with me and almost killed me. I can't explain it, but while my uncle and aunt were kneeling by my mother's broken body, I left my mother's womb and entered the womb of Aunt Monica, who became my mother by birth. Uncle Montel is actually my biological father and Alesandra was my mother."

The crowd was too stunned to speak. There was only harsh breathing and a loud moan as Pamela slid from her chair in a faint. At that, the crowd became unmanageable. Security was called to disperse the crowd and 911 was called for Pamela and others who were feeling faint. Some left quickly, just wanting to get away from the situation while others were overcome with curiosity and had to be herded out.

Montel sat in shock, not even moving when the paramedics lifted his mother to a gurney and wheeled her out. Cole walked toward Phoenix with anger and grief in his eyes. Monica sat sobbing, sure that Phoenix was having a mental breakdown. Trying to speak, to make sense of what he had heard, Cole choked when he tried to talk. He didn't know whether to hug Phoenix and comfort him or to angrily demand an explanation for his behavior. He finally reached toward Phoenix who stepped back and shook his head.

Eighteen Years and Seven Months Earlier

Montel and Alesandra, both skilled attorneys, were celebrating their fifth wedding anniversary. The day before, the doctor had confirmed that Alesandra was about six weeks pregnant. Dizzy with joy, the happy couple invited Montel's mother, his brother Cole and Cole's new wife, Monica to join them at the dinner theatre. They shared their wonderful news with the family and then with a few close friends who happened to be nearby.

Montel had received the call to come talk to his client in serious circumstances. He never turned down anyone who needed his help.

Cole and Monica had take Pamela home with them and Montel had run by the apartment to take Alesandra home. He had picked her up and swung her around, kissing her passionately. They were both laughing and loving each other so much when he left.

Montel was exasperated when no one showed up at his office. Wanting desperately to be with his wife and share their happiness, he hurried home.

He was devastated to find she had fallen from the balcony.

How could she have fallen? She didn't drink and certainly had no alcohol to blame. She was ecstatic with her pregnancy. She would never have thrown herself off purposely. Investigations went slowly and then the frustrating results -- unfortunate accident. Montel had almost lost his mind with grief.

He had finally agreed to go on the cruise with the family and was happy for Cole and Monica when they announced they were pregnant. He thought Monica and Alesandra must have conceived at about the same time. His despair at losing his beloved wife and unborn child almost did him in again, but family stayed with him and encouraged him.

After Monica gave birth, Montel had gone to see mother and the new baby boy. When he took the baby in his arms, the baby opened his eyes and looked straight up at him. Holy Hannah! The baby had violet eyes just as Alesandra had. Montel immediately felt a bond with this child. He was dear to his heart and he rejoiced in his years of growth and achievements.

Back to the Present, June 14

Now Phoenix had astonished and confused everyone with his announcement. He sat quietly at a table with Cole and Monica. Cole kept gulping as if he couldn't breathe and his eyes were puffed and red with unshed tears. Monica had stopped sobbing, but silent tears continued to run down her cheeks. With a heavy heart, Montel walked to them searching his brain as to what he could say to Phoenix.

Montel sat beside Phoenix and placed an arm around the young man's shoulders. "Phoenix, do you feel comfortable talking to me here, or would you rather go somewhere with me and talk privately? You do know we have to discuss what you've said. I'll admit, it's frightening, but we have to talk about it."

Phoenix looked sorrowfully at him and shrugged his shoulders. "Whatever you want. I don't mind talking here. It's got to come out eventually."

"I'm listening," Montel said softly and gave Phoenix a quick one-armed hug.

"Well, I'm not sure I can explain. If it had not happened to me, I would not have believed a word of it. I felt the joy my mother felt and knew both of you would love and welcome a baby with your whole hearts. Mother," he stopped and looked apologetically at Monica. She reached over and patted his hand with a loving, but strained smile. "Mother danced around and was so happy waiting for you to return. I can't explain how a six week old fetus knows these things. She answered a knock at the door and it was Grandmother. At first they were friendly, then Grandmother told mother that she must not have this baby because she had heard there was insanity in mother's family. Mother laughed and said there was nothing to that.

He sighed deeply using his fists to rub his eyes as a small child might. "Grandmother got angry and said mother's background was not as good as the Kennedys. She said that you," he looked at Montel, "were the oldest and her favorite because you looked like your father whom she adored. She had hoped you would stay at home with her. Mother was astonished but didn't get excited. She tried to calm Grandmother and reason with her. "

"Grandmother claimed to be feeling faint and said she needed fresh air. They walked out on to the balcony and, after a while, Grandmother kept moving until she crowded mother against the railing and pushed her over. Mother didn't die as soon as she hit even though just about every bone in her body was broken. I don't know where they came from," he nodded toward Cole and Monica, "but they knelt by mother and tried to comfort her. Somehow I left mother's womb and entered," he hesitated and bent his head, "hers."

Cole was shocked and spluttered trying to talk. "I would never have believed this except for one thing. Monica and I took mother home from the restaurant and sat with her. She ranted and raved over Alesandra not being good enough for her son and not good enough to carry a Kennedy. Mother went to her bedroom and I soon went to use the bathroom in the hall outside her room. As I passed mother's room, I heard her talking to dad's picture. She was telling him that Alesandra was not the same quality as the Kennedys and should not be allowed to give birth to a Kennedy baby. I didn't pay much attention to it except to be annoyed with her. When I returned to the living room, Monica said that mother had gone out and had walked by her as if she were in a trance. Monica spoke to her but she didn't answer."

Monica broke in. "Cole told me what he had heard Pamela say and I suggested that we drive by your apartment and see if Pamela had gone there. When we arrived, we found Alesandra on the sidewalk. We got through the crowd and knelt by her. She looked at me and tried to say something, but couldn't. At the time we didn't know she had fallen nine stories. Pamela was nowhere in sight and we didn't see her again until the next morning at the house. When we told her about Alesandra, she showed no sign of grief or curiosity."

At that moment, a family friend, Dr. Mitchell Miller, came and sat at the table with them. "I'm so sorry to bring you news such as this, but Pamela just seemed to not want to live. She gave up and her heart stopped about half an hour ago. I was present for the party and couldn't understand all this young man was saying. I suggest nothing more be said and I'm also suggesting counseling for Phoenix, and maybe all of you. What Phoenix said cannot be explained, but nothing surprises me any more. The manager is keeping the news media at bay in the front lounge. You might want to leave by the back door and I'll talk to the media -- if that's all right with you."

Cole and Monica nodded. Montel said, "I think you can handle them better than we can at this time. How could we explain what Phoenix accused his Grandmother of doing? I agree he needs counseling. Fortunately he leaves in a couple of weeks for college. He knows we all love him and will stand by him."

Dr. Miller smiled at Montel. "Is the scuttlebutt true? Are you going to marry Izabella? By the way, where is she?"

"She decided to go on home and let the family be together. She's the first woman I've felt attracted to since Alesandra's death. Yes, we've discussed marriage, but we have a lot of talking to do yet. I'm hopeful," Montel smiled weakly. "Thank you, Dr. Miller, for being with mother. She's known you for years and I'm sure she was comforted by you being by her. A sincere thank you for being willing to bear the media for us." Montel looked at Cole and Monica. "I guess Dr. Miller can tell them that Phoenix has been stressed over classes, tests, etc, and that he had a temporary breakdown." They looked at each other and nodded.

After Dr. Miller left, Cole and Monica stood and put their arms around each other. They reached out to hug Phoenix to them. Cole spoke in a shaky voice. "Son you **are** ours. We love you and will always love you. We'll always stand by you and help you any way that we can. Please feel free to come to me and talk about anything."

Phoenix hugged them separately and then turned to Montel. "Can I do home with you tonight? I don't want to talk to anyone. I just want to be by myself and think. I'm looking forward to training for an attorney. I'm sorry Grandmother died, but it was probably her time to go. I hope she can explain herself to God. I don't, and have never hated her. I love all of you.

"I'll have someone bring my car around to the back door. If it's okay with your parents, I'd love to have you stay with me as long as you need to," Montel said with a smile.

Monica hugged Montel and thanked him. "Yes, son, I'd rather you come home, but news people might follow us to our house and Montel lives in a well-guarded apartment building. We'll get together tomorrow." She and Cole hugged Phoenix again and left by the back door where someone had also brought their car.

Montel slapped Phoenix on the back. "Come on, son. Let's go home."

He sucked in a quick breath. "Yes, son, let's go home."

SHADOW MAN

It is *so* true. I told them so, but they won't believe me. I knew there were monsters. I saw him out there, but if I call daddy to come see, he'll go away and hide. He doesn't want big people to see him. I told the police I saw him when mommy died. They all said I was just scared.

Five year old Lida Millicent Featherstone held her breath and sneaked a peep out her bedroom window again. She stood to one side in case the Shadow Man looked up at her window.

The moon was shining but every now and then a cloud drifted across it and left the night a little darker. The bright street light kept the night from being entirely dark. Lida eased more to the center of the window, keeping low, and hoping to get a good view without being seen. Should she risk it and call someone to come look with her? Should she go out and try to catch the Shadow Man by herself? She frowned as she tried to decide what to do.

Seeing a motion out of the corner of her eye, her heart gave a leap of fear and her tiny body shook. Silly. That's me I see in the mirror. Slowly she turned to look out again, but --- there was nothing there. I **did** see him, I know I did. Didn't I? Maybe the grownups are right. Maybe it's all my magenashun."

Fearfully she climbed back into her bed and hugged her teddy bear tightly to her chest. Did the Shadow Man see me looking out? Will he come after me next and make me dead like he did mommy? She sniffled and made herself as small as possible.

Maxmillian Featherstone thankfully finished the brief he was writing to take to court the next day. He stretched his tired back and shoulders and yawned as he stood up. He walked over the house checking to see all windows and doors were secure. He pulled the drapes closed on the downstairs windows.

As he checked the French doors leading out to the patio, he looked carefully into the dark thinking he had seen a motion out there.

Is someone there and looking in or is the wind blowing enough to make the tree branches sway? Now I'm getting as bad as Lida. He chuckled to himself and then thought sadly of his little daughter who was having a terrible time accepting the death of her mother, Renee.

He thought of the night his wife had gone downstairs without turning on a light. She had called out that the kitchen light had been left on and she was going down to turn it off. He had heard her loudly say, "No!" and then heard a thump as she fell the last few stairs. Her neck was broken. Just a freak accident.

Lida had crept out without them knowing she was up. She had been sitting on the floor of the upstairs hall, looking through the railing, when her mother fell. He shook his head recalling that she had told the police a monster had caused her mother to fall --- a Shadow Man.

Darling little girl, so like her mother with long, black hair, violet eyes, long eyelashes and dimples with a perfect complexion. Both of his girls, wife and daughter, with cream and peaches skin and ready smiles had always been dear to his heart. He sorrowfully, and slowly, climbed the stairs trying to think of a way to comfort his daughter and help her to accept her mother's death and get over her fear of the so-called monster.

Max was one of the most successful attorneys in the city, even in the state. He now regretted working so many hours to achieve success and material possessions for his family as well as a good financial future for them. His wife and baby daughter were his heart. They were planning on another baby a year ago when the tragic accident had occurred. Now it was just him and Lida Mae. He was so thankful to have her. *She is a true blessing for me, my heart and my reason for going on.*

Easing into Lida's room, he gazed with a heart full of love at his little daughter. She lay in twisted bed clothes, a frown on her tiny face and a teddy bear clutched tightly to her small chest. He leaned over to gently kiss her cheek and carefully straighten the covers. *Oh, my little darling, I pray I can take that frown off your face and make your life peaceful and happy. I know you miss your mother, and I sure do, but with God's help we'll get through this sadness.*

Weeks passed and Max thought Lida was accepting the loss of her mother. He had moved some of his business into the house so he could be near for her. A wonderful housekeeper was a treasure that he appreciated.

Max asked his personal secretary to arrange a party for the office staff and all who worked with them. He felt it was time they had a friendly get together. The party was in full swing when the doorbell rang and at the same time the porch light burned out. The street light gave enough illumination for Max to recognize a senior partner in his firm.

"Clyde. I'm glad you could make it. Come on in. Is it raining yet?" he asked peering out.

"No. No rain, but the wind is rising. We'll have a storm and a half before the night is over."

As Clyde Marcum stepped through the door, everyone was startled to hear a piercing scream. Max jerked around in surprise to see Lida hanging on the railing half way down the stairs. Her eyes were wide in shock and tears were streaming down her cheeks.

"It's him! It's him, Daddy. Run before he kills you like he did mommy."

Embarrassed, Max ran to take Lida in his arms. He turned to his secretary who had run beside him. "Please see that the party continues and explain to the group how upset she has been since her mother's death. Clyde, I'm so sorry. I've told you how difficult it's been for Lida. She's overexcited because this is the first party we've had since the loss of her mother. The porch light went out just as you came through the door and triggered frightening thoughts for her. Forgive us. People, please go on with the party and enjoy yourselves. I'm taking my little angel to bed and will be down later." he smiled reassuringly at his daughter and carried her up to her room.

"But, Daddy," she protested, "that **is** the Shadow Man. He was hiding in the dining room and as mommy went down the stairs, he ran up the stairs to meet her and threw her down to the floor. He never saw me. When he heard you coming, he ran back into the dining room and I bet he went out the kitchen door."

Lida was only four when she lost her mother. She imagined a lot and has twisted memories with movies, I bet. She couldn't have seen that happen.

Mac calmed Lida and lay beside her on the bed. He remembered the kitchen door had been unlocked and even standing open a crack. He had thought they had just forgotten to lock it and it had blown open. There was no way that his partner, Clyde Marcum, would have even wanted to hurt Renee. Clyde was a wealthy man, well-known in the community and known for his generous philanthropy to the community. He had never married after the death of his wife, but had never seemed to be interested.

The following Monday, Max apologized again to Clyde and expressed his concern for his little daughter.

"You understand how devastating a death can be, especially to a little child. Your own wife was killed by a mugger on her way home from a concert. It was fortunate that my wife came out in time to see the man run away and she called for help. The police never found the perpetrator, did they?" Max looked with sympathy at Clyde.

"No. Unfortunately they didn't. It was kind of your wife to call for help and stay with her. The Medical Examiner said she had died almost immediately after being hit so hard on her temple. I hope she didn't suffer. They seemed to think she hadn't."

Max slapped Clyde on the shoulder and walked off. His thoughts were whirling like a hurricane, wondering how he could help his daughter. He would do anything he could for her, but he also had a business to take care of. He needed to work to support them. After all, he needed to plan for Lida's future.

The following Friday, Lida ask permission to go to the next block to a friend's house. She was excited about eating dinner and spending the night by herself like a big girl. It would be her first pajama party. She begged to be allowed to walk there like a big girl.

Max would miss her, but he wanted her to have a normal life. Too, it was encouraging to see her appear to be happy and at ease. It was daylight as Lida begged to go alone. Max hid out of sight and watched her go to the Henderson's and walk inside.

Max was sitting quietly catching up on some articles in law magazines when a commotion outside got his attention. A neighbor dog was barking wildly and several adult voices could be heard as if they were excited. He jumped up and ran outside to see what the disturbance was. He almost ran into his next-door neighbor as he hurried out his front door.

"Oh, Max. Thank goodness you're home. Now don't be frightened. Lida is fine and we have the man who tried to abduct her."

"Abduct her!? But she's spending the night with the Henderson's. What are you talking about?"

Max and his neighbor walked toward a group of neighbors just as a police cruiser pulled up. Two officers hurried out and quickly handcuffed a man that two neighbor men were holding.

Max ran to where a neighbor man had Lida in his arms. "Darling, what are you doing out here? Didn't you want to spend the night with Suzie?" He turned to another neighbor. "What's this about a man trying to abduct my daughter?"

Burleigh Carson spoke through the cacophony of excited voices. "My dog is the hero. I was walking Brutus and suddenly he jerked away from me and charged across the street. When I ran after him, Brutus had this man down and was going after his throat. Lida was on the ground in shock. I wasn't sure how badly she might be hurt."

Max looked puzzled at Lida. "Honey, why were you outside in the dark?"

"Daddy, I got worried about you. I had this awful feeling and thought you might need me. I was walking back home when the Shadow Man jumped out of the bushes and grabbed me. Brutus heard me scream and came flying over to jump on the man. I told you the Shadow Man was still around. I've looked out the window lots of times to see him sneaking around. He's always trying to see in our house. He's the one that threw mommy down the stairs."

"Let's see who this is," Max said to a police officer. The policemen had placed the man in the back of the cruiser.

The second officer turned a spotlight flashlight on the handcuffed man. Max gasped in surprise. "Clyde! There's got to be some mistake. What are you doing here? You don't live anywhere near here." Suddenly the light went on in his mind. "Lida did see you sneak into our house and kill her mother. Why, Clyde? Why?"

Clyde brazenly faced the hostile crowd. "The kid's mixed up. I was walking along and saw her trip and start to fall. I was just catching her."

"Oh, Daddy. You said it was a sin to lie. He's telling a lie. He was hiding in the bushes and jumped out and got me. He said, "Now you'll get what you deserve." He said that to me, Daddy. I screamed and Brutus ran over and jumped on him." She dropped to the sidewalk to hug the dog. "Good old Brutus. You're my real friend."

A woman neighbor took Lida and offered to take her home and get her settled. Max accepted gratefully.

Max glared at Clyde. "Why would you be walking more than five miles from your neighborhood? Now's a good time for you to tell the truth. It will come out anyway." Max looked as if he could tear Clyde apart with his own bare hands. His fists were clenched and he spoke through gritted teeth.

One officer apologized to Max. "The law states that he has the right to an attorney and that he doesn't have to say anything that will incriminate him. Many times we have to handle scum like this gently and give them all rights by law, when we would like to treat him as you obviously want to. None of us approve of dirt bags that will harm a child." He turned to the crowd. "Do all of us a favor and go home. There's nothing more to see here."

"Mr. Featherstone, a female office will be at your house in a few minutes to take a statement from your daughter. We need to get her impressions while it's fresh in her mind."

"All right. We'll be at my home. I'll fix hot chocolate for her and let her look at one of her favorite videos. I'm sure she's too high to get to sleep."

Max walked home with a heavy heart but thankful for a dog that saved his precious little girl.

"Am I in trouble, Daddy? Are the police going to rest me?"

"No, darling. They just want you to tell them what happened. Bad men get put in jail, not sweet, little girls."

The two female officers who came to take Lida's statement knew nothing about the case and couldn't answer Max's questions. Officer Dorsey wrote what Lida told her, even about seeing the man that killed her mother. She told them about the Shadow Man sneaking outside around the house sometimes at night.

After Officers Marian Dorsey and Melinda Burnside had left, Max looked at a Disney video with Lida and smiled with relief when she fell asleep against his side. She opened an eye when he kissed her cheek, but snuggled close in his arms and went back to sleep. He lay with her a while cuddling her in his arms and thankful that his little angel was safe.

Max called the police station, but was told that he would have to come to the station the next day to talk to whoever was in charge of the case. He was also informed that it was possible that only his attorney would be permitted to ask for the information and share it with him.

"Why would I need an attorney? My daughter, nor I, did anything wrong.

I'm an attorney."

"If this man can be proven guilty, you might want to pursue getting restitution from him or ensuring that he gets proper punishment."

Max thanked the person and hung up slowly with worried and angry thoughts. *Was Clyde really the one who killed my wife? For what reason? Lida is so sure he saw him and is sure of her identification. Did he truly intend to harm Lida?*

Clyde refused to talk to anyone except the attorney he had contacted.

Max was confused and frustrated. What reason could Clyde have for killing Renee? Why would he want to harm Lida? Was Clyde sane or had Renee found something about him that would be trouble for him?

During the trial, when Clyde finally realized he was going to prison, he agreed to answer Max's questions. Clyde was seventy-six and realized that he would not be comfortable in prison, or last long. He thought if he talked, he might get a break. Too, there were men in prison that he had helped send there and he knew how thrilled they would be to get hold of him.

Clyde, Clyde's attorney, Max and an impartial judge sat in a room to discuss what had happened. The judge was there to ensure that all laws were recognized and followed. Max was deeply hurt that Clyde had never offered an apology. He could hardly wait for Clyde to start talking. A Court Reporter was present to take a record of all conversation.

Clyde drew a deep breath and hung his head. He finally looked at Max. "None of you know how close I was to bankruptcy. I was deep in gambling debts and afraid the loan sharks would come after me. Jennifer and I had big insurance policies on each other, too she had not touched a two million dollar inheritance. When I ask her to help me, we had a fight and she refused. I hired a thug to mug her and kill her so that I could collect the money. I promised myself that I would never gamble again. Apparently Jennifer lived long enough to tell Renee about our disagreement and she thought I had hired the man to kill her. Renee came privately to talk to me about it, and I assured her that she misunderstood. I was afraid if she told someone, there would be those that believed her. I did throw Renee down the stairs and make sure her neck was broken."

"I thought I heard the little girl cry out, but wasn't sure until several days later you told me what she had seen and how disturbed she was. I decided that I wouldn't be safe until she was taken care of, also. I truthfully don't know what I would have done with her. I was so upset. I just wanted to take her somewhere and talk to her. I first thought I could convince her she just had some bad dreams, but when I took hold of her and she screamed, and the dog attacked me, I knew it was all over."

Max was too hurt to say anything. He had sat with clenched jaws, but now tears were running down his cheeks. He couldn't speak. Clyde's attorney said that was all and Max walked slowly out of the room. He just wanted to get to Lida and hug her.

A neighbor, Mrs. Perkins, had stayed with Lida. The housekeeper was too upset to work. Max thanked her for being with Lida and apologized because he didn't want to discuss anything. Mrs. Perkins understood, although she was curious. Mr. Perkins listened to his wife tell what Lida had told her and how Max had acted when he came home. He told his wife that Max was burdened with grief and they would find out later what happened. After all, Max had trusted a business partner and had lost his wife and almost lost his daughter. Too, he had liked Clyde's wife.

Max sat in shock throughout Clyde's trial. When he was sentenced to prison for life, Max sneered. He knew Clyde's life would be short, and he didn't feel Clyde would suffer enough.

Max spent a few months winding up the business in the office and selling his business and the goodwill with it. He reluctantly sold the house that he and Renee had planned together, but he wanted Lida to leave the bad memories behind with little to remind her of them. He and Lida moved to another state.

After a short period of time, Max applied and was permitted to open a law office. Lida was now in school and he had a full-time housekeeper who knew nothing of their troublesome past. He was relieved to see Lida laughing and making new friends. *Thank God she's young enough to forget the tragedy. I wish I could forget.*

Max's new secretary, and others, had tried numerous times to pair him with a woman friend. He quietly celebrated his thirtieth birthday and tactfully turned them all down. One day his secretary had brought some papers to the house for him to sign. Lida came rushing in.

"Daddy! Daddy! You ask me what I wanted for Christmas. I figured out what I want." The secretary hesitated in leaving and turned a loving smile on Lida wanting to hear what she desired for Christmas.

"What do you want, my angel?"

"I think I need a mother."

Shocked, Max looked at his secretary. She grinned and walked jauntily out the door. Lida was still talking and making plans for the holiday. She was excited as all youngsters get at the idea of the holidays. Max carefully explained how he really loved her. But was far too busy to hunt for a mother for her. He told her how important it was to find just the right one.

As days went by, Max thought Lida had put the idea aside because she didn't mention it again.

Lida demanded that Max take time to come see her in the Christmas program at school. She was to be a singing angel. Max was delighted and so proud of his daughter's singing and dancing. After the program, he went to her room for refreshments and to talk to other parents.

Max was talking to one of the fathers when Lida led her teacher to meet her daddy. The teacher, Miss Rosalie Martin, was attractive, vivacious and obviously loved by the students. She loved her job and her students. She excused herself to talk to other parents.

As Miss Martin walked away, Lida piped up with her childish voice, loud and clear. "Daddy, don't you think that Miss Martin would make a nice mother for me?"

Absolute silence fell on the room. Max stood with a very red face and, for once, was speechless. He choked on the punch and mumbling apologies, hurried Lida out of the room.

"Lida, how could you? Daddy is so embarrassed. Everyone heard what you said about ---" he stopped to make himself breathe.

"But Daddy. You're not married. Miss Martin isn't married, and she's so pretty and smart and sweet, and you're so handsome and smart and --"

"That's enough." he said firmly. "How can I ever face your teacher again?" He put her in the car, automatically clicked the seat belt around her and woodenly walked around to get in the car. He drove all the way home in silence. Lida was puzzled. *What did I say that was wrong?*

On the Saturday before Christmas on Tuesday, Rosalie was shopping in the mall and came face to face with Max. Both of them blushed. At the same time Max said, "Lida-" Rosalie said, "Lida -" They stopped and laughed.

"I'm so sorry that my little girl embarrassed you in front of the parents and students. I had no idea she was even thinking about it."

"Oh, don't apologize. I've worked with young children long enough to know they'll come up with strange ideas at the most inopportune time. As far as Lida's statement, she's been talking about it to me. She asked me if I would like to be her mother and I explained how busy I am. I also told her how a man and woman need to take time to get to know each other and have similar interests. She was interested in the idea of a couple dating and getting better acquainted. She told me she would tell you to date me.

Everyone thought it was charming. She is well liked and a very bright little girl."

"She's too bright, and I've always included her in everything I do. It has been the two of us for three years now. I have deliberately kept busy since we lost her mother in a shocking way. Then later I was horrified to find that my partner was responsible. He had killed his own wife, killed mine and was stalking Lida. I had hoped that time would help Lida get over the fright and grief."

"There's no need to explain. Lida has told me all that she remembers. You've done a superb job of raising her and letting her know how important she is to you. She can now talk about it without fear. Truly, I've learned to love her."

Max shuffled his feet like a teenager on his first date. "Would you like to give it a try? Go out together?" he ask hurriedly and nervously.

She smiled. "What did you have in mind?"

"How about we start with a dinner and getting to know each other?"

"Fine with me."

They agreed on the day after Christmas for a dinner at the Chateau.

Lida was elated, but not surprised, when Max and Rosalie announced their engagement on Valentine's day. Their wedding date was set for the fourth of July. Lida was in Seventh Heaven when they assured her she could be the flower girl and wear a big girl's long dress.

At the end of March, Max was notified that Clyde had died of natural causes. He was shocked to discover that he was Clyde's sole beneficiary. At first Max protested and said he wanted nothing of Clyde's, but then he thought about Lida losing her mother. He accepted with the understanding that everything would be placed in trust for Lida's twenty-fifth birthday.

Max's secretary smiled and silently eased out of the office motioning for others to be quiet. Max was sitting in his big leather chair, leaning back with his hands clasped behind his head and wearing a big, silly grin. He was a great boss and the entire staff was thrilled for him.

"All's well that ends well," a woman sighed.

"It hasn't ended yet," spat a disgruntled married man.

"It has as far as I'm concerned." They all jumped when Max spoke from the doorway. He was leaning against the door, hands in pockets, tie loosened and a goofy grin as the room erupted in cheers, whistles and applause.

MY CANINE HERO

I loved him. He was unbelievably ugly, suspicious and hard to live with, at first, but I did love him. I can tell you the story now that I'm past fifty and remember it well.

As a nine year old, I was a precocious youngster; very independent and knowing what I wanted. Oh, I was respectful to my elders and polite to everyone. That was something instilled in me from the time I was able to understand what was being said to me.

My daddy had inherited a fifteen hundred acre ranch from his father which had come down through the family from a great grandfather who had first come over from Scotland. There was enough money in the bank to keep it prospering, but, of course, money goes quickly, there, we had to work to keep everything going well.

Daddy bought some cattle that he began to breed for more lean meat and an animal that could stand the heat and drought conditions. He and his foreman, Paul Berring, worked hard and many hours a day. The hard work paid off. Daddy gave Paul and his family five acres to build on and have a garden of their own.

Horses were more interesting to me. I wanted to join a 4 H group and raise and show horses. I learned to ride both English and Western and caring properly for my babies. In fact, I lived in the stable more than I did in our home. What a joy! Even though it was a lot of hard work, and a lot of responsibility, I was walking on clouds and working hard to prove I could assume the responsibility.

The day of my tenth birthday, mom had invited classmates from school and children of our ranch workers for a party. Besides the great food, there were favors for each person present and a singing cowboy clown. One of the great movie stars, Roy Rogers, had shown up with his horse. Trigger, that did many tricks to entertain us. I received a load of presents from relatives and friends.

Being an only child was great, but there were times I longed for a sibling to confide in and share secrets. Sure, the workers children were friends and I enjoyed doing things with them, but it wasn't the same.

The day after my birthday I saw a car pull up at the end of the long driveway in front of our house. They didn't drive up to the house, which was suspicious. The opened a door and put something out. I could see it moving. Then they rushed off. I could see at least three people in the car.

I yelled at daddy, where he was putting some bailing wire on a truck, and started to run down the driveway. Mother rushed out and ordered me to stop and wait for an adult to go down and see about it. A few cowboys had come to the barn to do some work and heard me yelling. Two men came running to me. I pointed and told them what had happened. They jumped in a ranch truck and drove down that long driveway.

They came back holding a weird looking something. They handed it to me and I looked at the ugliest little puppy I had ever seen. He was light red with darker red spots, a head too big for his body and legs too short. His soulful brown eyes seemed to be begging for understanding and love. Paul said he probably wouldn't live because he was so deformed.

When those eyes seemed to be asking for help, my heart broke and I refused to let them put him down. Paul wanted to, as he said, put him out of his misery. I argued with them and ask how they knew he felt miserable.

Our veterinarian came the next day to give shots to some of the animals and I had him check the puppy. At first he laughed and said he'd never seen anything so strange. He thought the puppy might be about six weeks old. I took him to my heart and named him Speckles. The cowboys laughed at me and said dogs with spots like that were commonly called freckles.

Speckles he became and Speckles he was.

Speckles grew and was a faithful companion to me, but he didn't trust men in general and often hid from them. He would growl fiercely and show teeth. I have to admit that it was funny when he tried to learn tricks and commands. I told him all my secrets and the wishes of my heart. He never told a soul.

Sitting up was difficult for him, but he tried so hard. He would lie down on command and heel, but when I ask him to sit and shake hands, he would fall over. He sensed my love for the horses and developed a love of his own for them. He would follow them around the pasture and lie down with them in the spring sun.

Tornado weather became a problem in Nebraska, and I was afraid for my horses. One side of the pasture where I kept my horses, had a high mound on it. I had read of underground stables and begged daddy to dig out a section big enough for six stalls. He finally gave in and the work began. Of course, this was not something the cowboys were fond of doing and I got a lot of teasing as they worked.

The dirt was dug out and carried away to fill in some low places. Four by six posts, twelve feet tall, were used and strong timber to support a roof and build the stalls. Pressure treated wood was used in everything. I led the horses in and out of there every day so that they would not be afraid and maybe hurt themselves. I often led them in and fed them some grain. Speckles made every step with me and seemed to know what I was doing. He would sometimes herd them in there when he realized I was headed that direction. The horses were more relaxed and easier to handle when Speckles went with them. A quiet year passed and I excelled in 4 H and in open horse shows.

Tornado weather came with a vengeance. Property had been damaged close to us, but we seemed to be blessed when it passed all around us. One day the air was clear and the animals were moving calmly round the field. Suddenly Speckles ran to the house, barking and running around mother. She didn't know what to make of it, but decided to follow him. He led her around the house and to the storm cellar. She called on the range phone to daddy and told him what had happened. He said it was clear, but he would come to the house. He told the cowboys to be on the alert and to not risk their lives.

Speckles was ecstatic to see daddy come to the house and literally rounded us up and guided us to the storm cellar. Daddy laughed and said we might as well make it a rehearsal for the real thing. I took a book to read because there were kerosene lanterns down in the cellar. There was also bottled water, apples, raw turnips and quilts and pillows.

Daddy went up the steps to look out and exclaimed that a storm was building and maybe we were smart to be in the storm cellar. It wasn't long until the wind hit sounding like a freight train rolling over us. Daddy shut us in where we were safe.

I realized Speckles was not with us and demanded to be let out so I could get him. I cried until I was sick because daddy wouldn't even let me open the door and call. I cried even harder when I thought of my precious horses out in that dangerous storm. Daddy and mother both told me to trust and have faith in God.

Three hours later we ran out to discover our house demolished and ground and trees destroyed. The mailbox was gone for good. The fence between the house and the pasture was gone.

I ran out calling frantically for Speckles and the horses, naming them one by one. I ran into what was left of the pasture crying and calling. I heard a faint bark and ran toward it yelling for daddy to come with me. Dirt had blown in front of the opening of the underground stable. I could hear Speckles barking and the horses neighing.

The farm dogs had disappeared and we never found them except for one female expecting babies. Three of the cowboys came running and hurriedly brought the backhoe to us. They dug out the dirt that had covered the opening of the stable. There were the horses safe and sound and Speckles lying in a corner. We surmised that Speckles had rounded the horses up and drove them to safety. But what had happened to Speckles?

Speckles was just out of breath and tired. His little, short legs had traveled so hard and fast as they could to get the horses into safety. It had just been too much for his poor misshapen body. He was so glad to see me and licked my face all over when I gathered him up in my arms.

He died the next day and broke my twelve year old heart. Our veterinarian said we were lucky to have kept him this long. He said his heart had not been developed properly as it should have been and his little body couldn't take the stress of running and driving the horses to safety. I reminded everyone that he had saved us first.

Speckles was buried in the corner of the front yard with a flower bed in that corner to remind everyone of the brave, faithful little dog. He had learned to love us and trust us and had given his life for us.

We've had many fine, beautiful dogs since then, but none had a place in our hearts as much as that strange-looking little dog did. I wished many times I knew who had thrown him out so that I could thank them and tell them how much they had missed.

GOTCHA

Detective Ryan O'Malley crawled out of his beat up old Chevrolet in the hot parking lot behind the police station. He hadn't slept well and felt lower than a snake's belly. He absently patted the hood of the '89 Chevy that used to be a bright, green sedan. The old car was on its last legs, but he loved it and wanted to keep it as long as he could.

The usual greetings were called as he lumbered past officers leaving after night duty, and ambled into a room where others were drinking dark, rotten tasting coffee and munching on dried-up pastries.

Captain Marvin Simmons bounced into the room, his belly preceding him by a foot. In spite of his six feet, two hundred eighty-five frame, he moved with surprising grace. His bald head was already covered in sweat from the ninety degree heat. He was likeable, fair and thorough, but was a stickler for following the rules by the book. None of the officers were disrespectful to him, in fact, if ask, they'd say they truly liked him.

He greeted the men and women with genuine warmth, but puckered his face and refused a cup of their coffee. He discussed plans and orders for the day and made additional assignments on the breaking and entering that was becoming alarmingly regular. Dismissing them to attend to their duties, he smiled after them as proud as a father might his own children.

"Ryan," he called, "please come into my office. I'd like a word with you."

Puzzled, Ryan followed the Captain and sat in the chair that was pointed out to him. "Ryan, you've earned the name of being pertinacious (the Captain loved to use unusual words) and I'm sure it's condign. I'm going to assign you to undercover work that I'm sure will be accordant with you."

Ryan wanted to say, "Huh. Speak English." But having a college education and an extended education in criminal justice, he didn't want the Captain to think his vocabulary was limited. He sat quietly and looked at the Captain, hopefully showing some interest -- although he wasn't.

"Ryan, you're not what the ladies call handsome, but you have charisma and presence that attracts ladies. Let's see -- humm -- you're six-four, two hundred ten pounds, light brown hair, hazel eyes and longer eyelashes than a man deserves. Your tan shows up well and -- well, you're just what is needed."

Ryan wanted to shout, "Get on with it. What are you driving at?", but he sat quietly even though he felt itchy and restless. His skin seemed to crawl. He was suspicious of people who gave a lot of praise. That usually meant they wanted something from you that you wouldn't normally want to give.

The Captain went on, "We've had numerous complaints from patrons of a dating agency on Wicker Street. The clients pay a lot of money to be placed in the agency computer and then either get dud offerings or go weeks with no results. We need to know if these people are properly licensed and if they're being honest with clients. I want you to join, giving a false name and occupation. You'll be covered from here with the necessary information. I'll allow sixty days for you to ferret out the truth."

"Captain Simmons! I'm married. Suppose I come in contact with someone who knows me?"

"You're separated and I happen to know that your wife has filed for divorce. She says she didn't realize you would be away from home so much, or that you would be on call at any time and in so much danger. If she had known in advance, she says she wouldn't have married a policeman." He paused not even out of breath after saying this on practically one breath.

"Sir, I ---"

"No excuses. You're the man for the job. Go home, dress in a nice suit and be at the agency at eleven this morning. The owner comes in between eleven and two. I know you're polytheistic. You're good at reading people. Tell me what you think of her and any employees you meet."

With a heavy, and an angry, heart, Ryan excused himself and went to his desk to finish some paper work that had to be completed. He gave an absent-minded greeting to Chief Wilber Browning as the Chief paused at the door of Ryan's cubicle to greet him. Realizing Ryan was busy and engrossed in his work, the Chief walked on, smiling and greeting others.

Ryan reluctantly left to go back to his rented rooms and dress as the Captain had ordered. Whistling tunelessly, he flagged a taxi to take him to the other side of town. Sioux City, Iowa was a big city. His police station was at the north end of the city and the dating agency was at the southwest end. He found the agency with no trouble, but entered with trepidation.

Completing the personal interview, he was amazed that his answers were accepted without question. Several of the women, working there, made it their business to come by and get a good look at him. He overheard one woman say, "It isn't fair that, just because we work here, we can't take advantage of the services. I would claim him in a New York minute." The three women giggled and moved on.

Ryan was more than uneasy. For some reason the buzz of possible trouble, and the unknown, were running through his brain. It wasn't just the fact that he was still legally married, although he would have had trouble explaining it. Something bad was in the air. He could sense it just as clearly as if it were written on a poster on the wall.

Ryan met an office manager, a Mr. Toro Bernisky, who looked as if he could wrestle Hulk Hogan to the ground with one arm. The owner, a widow, Mrs. Hillary Barron, came in about eleven thirty. She had obviously dyed red hair, blue eyes (contacts?) and curves in the right places. Ryan was thirty-four, but he told himself, in the line of duty, he would date an older woman. He was secretly amused that she was flirting with him.

Finally he completed the interview, made his video tape and prepared to leave. His eyes had taken in more than the employees realized and his steel-trap brain had absorbed quite a bit. He grinned broadly when Mrs. Barron held his hand far too long and walked him to the door, promising to give him individual attention. Outside he lost his grin and began to go over what he had seen, heard and observed. That strange, itchy feeling still crawled between his shoulder blades. He commonly felt this when he was on a stake-out.

He debated with himself whether he should go by his house and get some of his clothing that he had left when he moved to the apartment. No. Jonell might be at home and would accuse him of trying to get back with her, or worse, accuse him of spying on her. He didn't want the hassle.

Regardless of the reasons she stated for wanting a divorce, he was suspicious that she might be seeing another man. Frankly, he didn't care. In their four years of marriage, she had been a true wife to him only the first few months. She went on lengthy trips and spent more money than was necessary.

Jonell's father, as mayor of the city, had a lot of political influence. He was involved with a lot of big-shot politicians. It was rumored that he might try for governor of Iowa the following year. Ryan got along well with Dewey Chandler, but had no desire to be buddy-buddy with him.

Mrs. Chandler had died when Jonell was ten, and her daddy had spoiled her rotten. They were not rich like Trump or Gates, but were very well off. Mayor Chandler had paid for companions and anything else Jonell wanted so he wouldn't have to bother with her. She was on her own at a far too young age. She had lacked for nothing. Her daddy was livid when he learned she was asking for a divorce. It just wasn't done in their family and he was afraid it would hurt his political aspirations. But Ryan couldn't think of Jonell and her daddy now. He had work to do. It was always risky going undercover. Being discovered could mean a sound beating or even death.

Ryan wasn't surprised when he was informed in two days that a match had been found for him at the dating agency. He went to the agency to view the tapes of the women who had selected him. He was to view the tapes and decide if he wanted to meet either of them. He asked for time to think it over.

On his way out, he looked to the left when a door to a room opened. He was astonished to see Mayor Dewey Chandler standing in the doorway looking back to talk to someone in the room. He was laughing and very much at ease. Ryan quickly ducked out hoping his father-in-law had not seen him.

Mulling over his discovery, Ryan reported to the Captain and met with the newly hired secretary, Bernice Hartley. She was a vivacious young woman of about twenty-six. About five-five, one hundred ten pounds, she exuded a love of life and joy at being allowed to work with the police. Her short, curly, golden blonde hair and soft green eyes were set off by a beautiful complexion. She smiled continuously and was so pleased to be working where she was, that she bounced when she walked.

Bernice confided in Ryan that she had her heart set on being included in a case some day, hoping to become an officer and finally a detective. She giggling confessed that she had read all the Nancy Drew mysteries and the Hardy Boys as a teen. She watched all the Perry Mason and Matlock films. He looked seriously at her while she talked, but inside he was bursting to laugh out loud. Oh, well. She was sweet, eager and qualified for the secretarial position.

One Monday morning, coming to work early, he was perplexed to see most of his fellow officers in the front room looking strangely at him. No one was drinking the vile coffee or talking in groups. There was a strange pall on the air. Detective Ellen Carpenter walked to him looking as if she would rather be any where but here. She was usually a 'tough as nails' cop but this morning she looked as if she might burst into tears. Captain Simmons stood in the background, stern and yet looking at Ryan as if he pitied him.

Detective Carpenter walked to Ryan and said, "Detective O'Malley, it pains me to have to do my duty and place you under arrest for the murder of your estranged wife, Jonell Chandler O'Malley."

Ryan was too astonished to say anything for a few seconds. "Jonell is dead?! How? When?" he sat down heavily and put his face in his hands. "I haven't seen her in over two weeks. Why would you think I would kill my own wife, even if we are separated?"

Captain Simmons walked to stand in front of Ryan. 'She called me last week and said she thought you were stalking her and she was afraid of you. We paid no attention to it then because she was always trying to cause trouble for you. But now ---"

Detective Carpenter gave him the Miranda and said, "You need a lawyer with you when we give the evidence against you. Why am I telling you?

You know all of this better than I." She ran trembling fingers through her wavy, black hair. Her grey eyes were so sad that Ryan felt sorry for her, momentarily forgetting his own troubles.

Ryan was too numb with shock to protest when the Captain took his badge, ID, belt and weapon, laces from his shoes and his tie. He was placed in a separate cell from the other inmates. He sat on the narrow, hard cot for almost two hours trying to assimilate his situation before he thought to ask for an attorney. The majority of his fellow officers had been by to assure him they didn't believe he was guilty.

While Ryan was waiting for Attorney Robert Gibbs to arrive, Mayor Chandler came to see him. He vehemently assured Ryan that he did not believe Ryan was guilty. "They'll find it was one of those breaking and entering crimes we've had for several weeks. Or, I hate to say this, one of Jonell's men friends. Yes, I knew she was seeing several men. She must have ticked someone off. I feel guilty because I recognize that I'm partly responsible for her behavior, for spoiling her," Mayor Chandler told Ryan.

Ryan didn't answer the Mayor because he agreed with him. If he had started talking, he might have said more than was good for him considering his position.

The Mayor left as Attorney Gibbs rushed in, horrified that Ryan would even be accused. They were fortunate to obtain a hearing before Judge Earl Oliver and get Ryan out on bail. Gibbs finally became angry with Ryan and bawled him out because he moved and talked like a man in a trance. "Get a grip on yourself. You must get your brain working and think. I can't protect you completely unless you cooperate and work with me to reason this out. When did you speak to her last? What did you discuss? Have you seen or heard from her since you accidentally ran across her in the restaurant? How long has it been since you've been to the house? Were you with anyone who can vouch where you were yesterday afternoon? You do realize IA (Internal Affairs) will be investigating this also, don't you?" He shot question after question to a silent Ryan.

Jonell's vicious tongue and hate for his career had killed all love for her, but Ryan had been faithful in his marriage and didn't want to see her life snuffed out in such a horrendous way. Attorney Gibbs had informed him that Jonell had been choked and stabbed.

Following procedures, Ryan was placed on leave with pay until his trial.

This meant he could not go to the dating agency. He felt badly about letting the Captain down with his undercover investigation. It would be next to impossible for another officer to complete the investigation. By now the people at the agency knew who he was and they'd be on guard.

The five weeks that followed would have been unbearable except for Bernice and Ellen. Detective Ellen Carpenter had visited to tell him that no way would she believe he was guilty.

Bernice felt deep in her soul that he was innocent. She visited often and began to get annoyed with him because he sat and did nothing; just stared in space. He wasn't eating or cleaning himself up.

She came in one morning, slammed the door and threw her coat across the room. "I'm going to cook and you're going to eat. Then you're going to shave, take a shower and dress with self respect as you've always done."

He finally slowly moved his head around to look at her. He just stared for a few moments. "What?"

"You heard me. Come on, get to it."

"Go away. I'm doing just fine."

"No, you aren't. You should be ashamed. You are well educated, certainly have a lot of friends that believe in you. Even the Chief feels that you are innocent. You know as well as anyone that there are procedures that must be followed. It'll take a little time."

"Are you through?"

"No, and I'm not giving up. Ryan, you have so much to offer the world and it would be a sin for you to give up and let them railroad you."

"You really and truly believe I'm innocent?"

"I sure do and all the force thinks so, too. We know you're going to beat this regardless of whatever they try to pin on you."

Ryan sat and thought a little bit more, then slowly got up and went to his bedroom. A half hour later he came back into the living room, shaved, showered and dressed.

"Hooray!" Bernice cheered. "Now sit down and eat something sensible and let's plan what we're going to do next."

"We?"

"Yes, we. Ellen and I are going to work in your behalf as much as we can and several of the officers have volunteered even on their own time."

Ryan didn't say anything. He sat down and ate what Bernice had prepared. After he finished, he thanked her and looked more alive.

"Now, what do you mean -- planning?"

"Well, Ryan, all of us know you are innocent. We have to sit down and write out where you have been, with whom and what times, for the past month. It won't be easy, but your future is at stake. Take this calendar and I'll bring this pad and pen. Let's sit at the dining table and - go to war."

"I guess it will be easier to go backward. I'll start the day I was told I was under arrest and go back."

The two of them worked for almost two hours. Fortunately Ryan could account for a great deal of his time because he was working undercover at the dating agency. He also had a medical and a dental appointment. He gained courage as they worked because he was going to be able to account for a majority of his time.

Bernice had written the day and time of Jonel's death. 'What were you doing on that day? How long had it been since you had seen her or had any contact with her?"

"I had not seen her in about two and half weeks before she was killed.

She had called and left a message for me to call her about four days before that, but I never returned the call."

"And when you saw her before, it was in a restaurant in front of dozens of people. You ran into her accidentally. Right?"

"Yes, that's right. She yelled out then that I was avoiding her."

"Good. We'll see if we can't find someone who heard her and will be willing to testify as to what she said. Do you know any of the men she was seeing? Let me rephrase that.

Have you heard the names of any of the men she was seeing?"

"No, but her father knows. Maybe someone should ask him and then interview those men."

"Great idea. I'll make sure someone talks to Mayor Chandler and hopefully he'll give us some names. Some of the officers that volunteered will be glad to talk to them when we find them. Now we're getting somewhere," she cheered.

While they were talking, Ellen came in. "Hey, you two. You look like the cat that swallowed the canary. I hope it's good news."

Bernice brought her up-to-date on what they had started working on.

Ellen was thrilled.

"Let's make a list of things to do and I'll help with what I can. I'm sure some of the guys will be more than willing to help. They all realize that it could happen to them at any time."

Bernice came to Ryan's house every day to cook and make plans. He was beginning to take heart and get excited. A week later Ellen ran in after work.

"Guess what! I have a list of six names that Mayor Chandler reluctantly gave Bill Gannon."

"Sgt. Gannon?" Ryan asked surprised. "I didn't think he even liked me."

"He likes you well enough. When did you ever see him being too close with anyone?" Ellen asked. "You probably don't know that he had a wife who ran out on him and took his two year old son. She married the man she was running around with and took the boy too far away for Bill to visit. She was supposed to send the boy to him for certain visits, but that stopped after she and her new husband moved away. He's hurting, too, and he understands."

Bernice and Officer William Glover interviewed a few of the men and hit, what they considered, pay dirt. She ran back to tell Ryan and Ellen bringing William with her.

William was so excited, he wouldn't let anyone else talk. "I think we've got something mighty important. Jerry Stern was seeing Jonell on the night that she was killed. He hid out in another room when her father came to see her. He said Mayor Chandler yelled the roof off about her running around on you, about her getting a divorce and about her ruining his life as well as hers. Her old man had said, 'the world would be better off with you dead' and he stalked out."

Bernice spoke up. Jerry was so frightened of the Mayor that he crawled out a window and ran. He had planned to never go back, after all, he knew it was your house. We need to pin the Mayor down now and we need to be sneaky about it."

After much discussion and planning, they all agreed on a great plan. Ellen and William would make an appointment to see the Mayor and tell him what they had all decided on. The appointment was made for three the next afternoon.

"Hello, your Honor," William greeted the Mayor with a big smile and a glad hand.

"Hello, Mayor Chandler," Ellen was equally as pleasant. "We need to discuss some interesting news with you. I'm sorry it concerns the death of your daughter."

He hung his head and looked as sad as a kicked puppy. He looked at her. 'Talk away. I'm listening."

William took over. "We've been talking to the men on the list you gave us and much to our surprise, one of the men was hiding in a back room in the house when she was killed. Do you want to tell us about that, Mayor?"

Mayor Chandler looked as if he would faint. "I guess it's no use. I might as well confess. Yes, I did it."

William and Ellen both gasped. They hadn't expected this. They had no idea he had killed his own daughter. They were just going to get him to admit her checkered background to lay a foundation for Ryan's case.

Ellen kept a stoic expression. "Go on, sir."

"I did go to talk to her about the deplorable life she was living. She had been drinking too much and grabbed up a knife to stab me. We fought over the knife and it, somehow, ended up in her chest. She was screaming that she would have me thrown in jail and grabbed at my tie. It was loose and came off. I grabbed it from her and the next thing I knew it was around her neck and she was dropping to the floor. When I realized she was dead, I panicked and ran. Previously I had seen Ryan in the dating agency and thought he might have seen me. If word had leaked out that I was a partner there, it would have hurt my political chances. I hope Ryan will forgive me, but I let him take the fall."

William was taping all of this, but knew it could not be used in court. "Mayor, I've taped everything that was said here this afternoon. I'll take this to the station and have it typed in triplicate and you can sign it. You're very wise to go ahead and confess. It will go much easier on you.

Remember, everyone knew Jonell and how she was conducting herself."

Out in the car Ellen reminded him the tape couldn't be used in court. The Mayor was so upset he came right on down and signed the confession which made it legal.

Ryan was reinstated and soon had a promotion and a raise. He was so grateful to Ellen, Bernice and William and the other officers that had helped. They finally yelled, "Enough!" at him when he thanked them all over and over.

Ryan made sure Bernice got to go on some investigations with them. Ellen resigned to raise a family. Bernice and Ryan started dating and ten months later were married.

Bernice went to school and received the training necessary to pass her tests and become an officer. In two years she made detective. She was thrilled and walking on clouds.

On their third wedding anniversary, Ryan had taken Bernice on a long cruise. They returned in time to go to a party for the Chief's retirement. Captain Simmons was promoted to Chief and William was promoted to Captain.

After the retirement party, Bernice and Ryan came home thankful to get to bed and rest. Lights were out and all was still.

"I hope you're good at thinking of names, Daddy." Bernice whispered.

"Umm," Ryan replied sleepily. "What?!" he yelled turning on the light.

"I had my check-up today. I waited to tell you until I was sure. We're pregnant and it's going to be twins."

"Why don't you just hit a man in the head," he grinned. "We're really pregnant!? And it's really twins?" He whooped so loud in glee that he fell out of bed. Laughing, despite the late hour, they started calling family and friends to share the good news.

"See," Bernice said kissing Ryan tenderly, "all good things do come to those that wait in faith and patience."

THAT'S MIKEY

The quartet of my male cousins, with tears in their eyes and hearts, finished a beautiful rendition of "Vacation in Heaven" which followed "His Eye Is on the Sparrow" as the sun cast a benediction through the stained-glass windows of the church.

People in the congregation must have thought I was unfeeling and unusually calm. They had no idea how hollow I felt. My heart ached until I felt that could surely see my grief as if it were paint on my face.

My baby brother was in that coffin in front of us. My baby brother that I had raised and, in reality, had been big brother, mother and father to him. Life was taken from him when terrorists tortured and then killed him just as they had done to other hostages taken in Iraq. Let people think what they please. My grief and my memories are my own. He smiled as he thought.

March 1979

Seventh grade was a joy. I not only had had a wonderful twelfth birthday party, but I, Andrew Rutherford, had been selected to sing lead parts in our school operetta. It was a popular musical and I was willing to shed blood to be chosen. In fact, I had been chosen over some upper classmen. I knew dad would be pleased but mom would be ecstatic. Music, baseball, fishing with dad and camping with my family were my delights. I was mediocre in baseball, even though I loved to play. I excelled in singing and playing the piano and guitar which filled my soul with delight.

The day seemed longer than usual because I was anxious to get home and share my great news. After school I went across to the elementary building to get my eight year old sister, Susan Elaine, who was in the third grade. Eager to get home, I walked too fast for Susan, but she didn't mind. She was the family dreamer and was poking along enjoying the neighbors' flowers and chatting with anyone, or anything, that would listen --- old people, nosy neighbors, squirrels, birds and you name it.

Turning a corner, and coming in sight of home, I broke into a run. Racing down the sidewalk, I felt as if I were floating through the air with happiness. I began to sing and leap like a ballet dancer. I could see our white picket fence with flowers planted along the inside. Leaving the front gate swinging, I ran up the steps, across the wide porch and skidded to a stop with surprise as I bounded through the front door. The music stuck in my throat.

Dr. Morgan and two neighbor ladies stood in the hall. "Poor little lamb," said Mrs. Burton. "Come to the kitchen, dear. There are fresh-baked cookies and milk for you."

"Where's Susan? Aren't you supposed to be taking care of her?" These questions were asked over the shoulder of Mrs. Hayes as she looked anxiously out the front door. I began to taste fear. *Why was Mrs. Hayes looking so concerned? Why was Mrs. Burton wringing her hands looking as if she would like to cry?*

Mrs. Burton put her arm around my shoulders and led me into the kitchen. I followed because we had been taught to respect and obey the neighbors and the adults we knew. Mrs. Hayes soon led Susan into the kitchen where I had a good start on the cookies. I wanted to ask a lot of questions, but the expressions on the womens' faces kept me quiet.

Dad shuffled in and sat down by me. We were surprised to see him home from his lumber and hardware store. He didn't usually get home until between six-thirty and seven and it was now only three-thirty. As young as I was, I realized Dad looked strained and older than his forty-five years.

"Daddy," Sharon stood by him. "Why is Dr. Morgan here? Is mother upstairs? Is she real sick?" Trust Susan to get straight to the point. She always talked quick and perky.

"Yes, dear," dad answered placing an arm around Susan. "Mother is upstairs very sick. We must be quiet and let her rest. Dr. Morgan is here to take care of mother and to deliver your little brother that God sent to us this afternoon."

"A baby!" Susan screamed with delight. "Can I see him now? Can I play with him?"

"May I--" dad said absentmindedly. *Why was dad looking as if he was going to cry? He looked so sad and frail that I wanted to hug him, but I didn't.*

I sat with a cookie in one hand and thinking of what mother and dad had told me last Christmas. Susan thought mother was getting fat, but I noticed it was her stomach getting bigger. When I ask about it, my parents told me God had placed a baby in there for mother to take care of until it was big enough to be a new member of the family. They cautioned me not to discuss it with Susan because she was too young to understand. I ask if it would hurt mother to take the baby out when the time came. They told me sometimes it did but mothers expected to hurt a little, but it wouldn't last long.

Dad walked up to the second floor with us. We tiptoed into our parents' bedroom. Dad had to hold Susan to keep her from jumping on the bed and landing on mother. Susan gave a quick, wet kiss to mother and then raced to look at the baby. He was in a swinging crib that dad had made and painted it white when I was born. Mother had made a cute quilt. Each square had a colorful bird on it and white lace was sewn all around the edges.

I solemnly stood by the bed and gazed at mother, my heart twisting because she was so pale and damp with weak perspiration. "Are you okay?" I whispered fearfully to her.

"Yes," she spoke softly. "I expect you to help your daddy take care of Susan. And, son, your little brother will need you a lot to help him learn all the great things little boys do." Her voice was so weak she didn't sound like mother. I nodded seriously, looking calm, but couldn't speak around the knot in my throat.

Mrs. Burton had taken the shrieking, excited Susan out with her with the promise that Susan could help prepare dinner.

I sat in a rocking chair while dad placed a warm, soft bundle in my arms.

Looking with wonder at the small pink face, I felt a tenderness start in my heart and a lump came in my throat. I was too young to express myself, but mother and dad told me later that it made them feel good to see the expression on my face. They knew I was accepting my little brother with deep love.

With one finger I lightly touched the little round head with the soft wisps of dark hair. My heart lurched as violet eyes opened and seemed to look straight into mine. From that moment we were bonded. David Michael was mine.

The years seemed to pass so quickly. Mikey was a loving little boy who learned quickly and was always healthy. It almost took a small army to keep up with him. He was my shadow, most of the time, but when I needed to find him, it was a real task.

Late Summer, 1983

Holy mackerel! The last game of the season and I really had to concentrate. Our team was on top by one inning. We would either win the baseball trophy or tie. We wanted to win because our team had not won a season in our county in five years.

Susan and Mikey were in the bleachers loudly cheering for our team, and especially for me. Ordinarily a sixteen year old boy would be embarrassed by younger siblings, but I loved my sister and brother and felt very protective of them. Too, I was very proud of them and to be their brother.

I was considered the stable, reliable, no-nonsense, musically talented one. Twelve year old Susan was a tender, compassionate, artistic young girl. Four-year-old Mikey was a jester and a ray of sunshine to everyone he met.

On deck, waiting for my turn at bat, I smiled thinking of Mikey's statement the night before. After supper our family was watching a movie special when a commercial came on. A man yelled, as commercials do, "A single flea can lay hundreds of eggs to be a problem in the future."

Mikey listened intently and then turned to dad very serious. "Dad, if a single flea can lay hundreds of eggs, how many can a married flea lay?" We were laughing so hard we almost missed the last part of the movie.

Snooty Mrs. Pierpoint visited mother often. She was always laughing until she lost her breath at things Mikey would say. She told everyone at church and in the women's circle what Mikey said. She forgot to be hoity-toity and actually whooped loudly when Mikey ask what she and mother were talking about. He always misunderstood and had to have it explained. He would then say, "Well, that isn't funny."

My turn at bat. Con-cen-trate. Stare down the pitcher. It felt good. I swung. **Contact!** I brought in two players who were on bases ahead of me and I was right behind them. Home run! My friend, Danny Norris, made another home run right behind me. The next person was the third out, but it made no difference. We had won ten to six. The whole town celebrated.

The coach took us all to a pizza parlor to do our celebrating. How excited I was. Lynn parson, the most beautiful and most popular, girl in school was on my arm. I was 'walking on clouds due to our trophy win and my date with Lynn. It was better than a party.

None of the guys dared to tease me. I was easy-going and generally well-liked. I already stood six-one and had the weight to go with it. As much as I liked Lynn, my goal of college kept me from doing anything stupid to knock me out of it. I made sure Lynn understood that I wasn't ready for anything serious. I was relieved that she felt the same way and was also planning on a college education.

Dad took our family out to dinner the next night and invited Mr. & Mrs. Hayes and Mr. & Mrs. Burton to come with us. Mrs. Hayes kept us entertained telling of being invited to a high society home for dinner a few days before. The butler had false teeth that clicked when he talked.

With a solemn expression, dad asked, "Is that what you would call an indentured servant?" Did anyone wonder where Mikey gets his mischievous nature? Mikey had to have the joke explained to him. The way Mikey said, "That's not funny," had everyone laughing.

Mother was never a good joke teller. She usually said, "Have you heard the one about?" and then she'd tell the punch line. Now she started telling about the young preacher who went to a mountain community to hold revival services. An elder woman would stand up in the back and yell, "Amen. That's right, preacher, you tell 'em." every time he mentioned a sin.

He talked of drinking, gambling, smoking and telling lies with the old woman supporting him at each 'sin'. Then the preacher started telling how dipping snuff was a sin. This old woman stood up and angrily bustled out loudly proclaiming, "Now he's quit preaching and gone to meddling." Everyone smiled politely, and, again, Mikey had to have it explained to him. Even the people at the tables around us laughed when Mikey loudly stated, "You people just can't tell good jokes."

Feeling rather grown up, I was preparing to enter my senior year of high school. I still sang in the church youth choir and in the school glee club. My time was filled and stretched thin with music, sports, school and church.

Susan was losing baby fat and showing promise of becoming a very attractive young woman. I was so proud of her because she had won several art awards and kept on the top honor roll. I was also worried about her being a teenager and having to face peer pressure that I knew was there. Our parents were loving, but strict, and I knew she would have good home training to help guide her, but there was still a lot of exciting temptations. I strongly felt the responsibility of being the older brother.

Mikey was -- still Mikey. He had been feeling pretty big since he had entered kindergarten. All of us had known how to read and count when we entered school, therefore, Mikey was making top grades. He learned quickly and had a surprisingly mature vocabulary, but he was still our clown and con artist. He wrapped all of us around his finger. I don't think he did it intentionally, he was just a natural born charmer who loved people and the attention he got. He had a keen curiosity about many things and often astonished adults with his intelligent questions, and he was full of questions.

Mikey came home from school one day with a pensive expression. Mother asked him if he needed to talk about anything.

"Yes," he said seriously, "what does extinct mean?"

Mother patiently explained about the early giant animals that were no longer on Earth. She laughingly stated that if everyone in the world disappeared, then the human race would be extinct.

Mikey looked at her a second and said, "Well, but who would I say the word to then?"

Mother laughed and said, "He who gets too big for his britches will be exposed in the end." This set Mikey into gales of laughter and he repeated this until we were sick of hearing it.

A few nights later we were watching a special on National Geographic showing a hyena mother being killed and leaving babies. Another female hyena carried food in her mouth to feed the orphan babies until they were old enough to be taught to hunt for themselves.

The next day Mr. Burton had gone in his back yard to see why the neighbor's dog was barking, snarling and throwing a fit. He almost had a heart attack as he climbed, crawled and fell over the fence to grab Mikey to safety just in the nick of time. The mother dog has been ready to tear Mikey's face off as he crawled toward her babies with food in his mouth. Needless to say, Mikey received a stern lecture and a warm behind.

"But, Mother, I wanted to feed the babies," he sniffed and hiccupped looking as if he had been done a great wrong.

Mother patiently explained that the mother dog fed her babies herself from her own milk and didn't need help from humans or other animals.

"Well," Mikey pouted, "I couldn't find any orphans."

I noticed that mother was sick a lot and stayed in bed most of the time.

Dad looked worried and was acting so suspicious that I caught on. Mother was pregnant again! As soon as I was old enough to understand, Dad had explained that mother had a hard time carrying Mikey and Dr. Morgan had warned her not to have any more babies. I was horrified. Mother was forty-two and dad was - my gosh - dad was fifty-two.

I was furious with dad. I knew I went too far but I blessed him out good for putting mother through this again. Wonder of wonders, he didn't argue with me or answer me. Guess he was feeling too guilty.

It hurt that there was a break between dad and me. I had looked up to my parents and it was a shock, along with growing pains, to discover that dad was no longer my hero.

The end of that summer was hot and miserable. One Saturday night dad took our family out to dinner. Some people from our church were sitting at the next table and were glad to see us. One of the ladies came over and hugged Mikey. "What would you like, dear, a little brother or a little sister?"

"A hamburger," Mikey answered truthfully.

The adults continued to talk about other people they knew, but I was not paying attention. I noticed how tired mother looked. It finally penetrated that dad was talking about feeling tired and getting old. Dad looked hurt when the others laughed with him and I glared at him.

The days drug by and mother got worse. Dad hired a widow in our church to help with the housework, but I jealously took care of Mikey and Susan.

One day, as I brought my siblings home from a festival in the city park, Mrs. Burton and Mrs. Hayes met us on the walk in front of our house. I felt grateful for their years of friendship and caring, but did notice that they were really aging.

"Andy, I would like to take Mikey in with me for some cake I baked this afternoon. I'm sure I can find some ice cream to go with the cake," Mrs. Hayes said. She tried to smile, but I noticed that her eyes looked sad. I knew something was wrong as both women nodded at me and hurried Mikey into the Hayes house.

With lead-weighted hearts, Susan and I went into our house. Dad was coming down the stairs. "Son, your mother is real sick. She needs for us to be strong and pull together for her sake." For the first time in weeks, dad and I hugged each other.

"Is it all right if I go up to see her?" I ask as dad hugged Susan.

Dad nodded and Susan grabbed my hand to walk up with me. I knew Dr. Morgan was there because I had seen his car parked at the curb. We had only gone up two steps when we heard a vehicle stopping in our driveway. I was shocked to see an ambulance.

"Dr. Morgan says he needs to have mother where he has all of the necessary equipment and nurses to help. Mother's going to the hospital," Dad said sorrowfully.

I dropped Susan's hand and raced up the stairs, two at a time, to my parents' bedroom. Mother was gasping for breath and could hardly open her eyes. Her fingers lightly touched my cheek as I leaned over to kiss her cheek. We had always been so close, maybe because I was her first born.

"Take care of Susan and Mikey for me," mother whispered. "Help your dad. He truly loves you so much and is very proud of the man you're becoming. He needs you now - both of you," she reached to include Susan.

Susan sobbed and hugged mother promising to help.

Susan and Mikey were left at home with Mr. and Mrs. Burton. Dad and mother's youngest brother, David Bolling, took me to the hospital with them. David Michael was named for our Uncle David. That's why he was called Mikey. There was already a David.

I had to stay in the waiting room with Uncle David while dad went with mother. I was not ashamed of my tears, but I was upset to find I could not pray as I wanted to. I was numb and felt as if I were suspended in space.

Uncle David walked down the hall. When he returned and placed his hand on my shoulder, I knew the news was bad. "It was a little boy, but he couldn't make it," he said with a catch in his throat. "They're still working with Amelia. She's in bad shape."

Amelia? It's funny but I never thought of her having any other name but mother. About twenty minutes later another doctor came in and whispered something to Uncle David. He sat stunned and then put his head down and sobbed aloud. I knew, without being told, my mother was dead.

When dad, looking like a zombie, stumbled into the room, he held his arms out to me. One part of me wanted to hug him and cry with him, but my bad side took over. "YOU killed my mother," I exploded. I was astonished when dad fell to his knees and sobbed aloud.

The stone on the grave read: Amelia Sue Bolling Rutherford, beloved wife and mother. The angels rejoiced to welcome her to Heaven. The dates showed her to be forty-three.

I was cold to dad and only spoke to him when it was absolutely necessary.

At that time I didn't know that it would regret it for the rest of my life and would have to live with shame. Two weeks, after mother was buried, dad was laid to rest beside mother. Granville Lee Rutherford, at fifty-three, killed by drunk teenagers who crashed into his car when they ran a red light. I was crushed and ashamed that I had not comforted dad after the loss of his precious wife

Dad had planned well for the future of his children. Uncle David was to run the store on salary. If he did not wish to do so, he, and dad's attorney, were to select someone that they trusted to manage the store. Profits were to be divided in half. One half going back into the store and one half to be used for his children.

Mother had an inheritance from her maternal grandfather that she had never touched. It had gained interest through the years and was to be used for her children's education.

Susan became a mature, young woman far too early. She proved to be a capable helper to the woman who had been hired to care for us. Mrs. Catherine Findley was a widow who was pleased, and relieved, to have the job. She was tall and thin with graying hair pulled back in a bun that never seemed to move. Her gray eyes twinkled and she truly loved and cared for us. Mikey had not yet felt a great loss of his parents. Besides, I had always been there for Mikey and still was.

Now I was seventeen and had my drive's license. It made it easier on everyone. I could run a lot of errands and take my siblings where they had to be. I felt the responsibility and wanted to stay home to work in the store and help at home. Uncle David wouldn't hear of it. He reminded me that both parents had their hearts set on us getting a college education.

Uncle David and Aunt Cecelia wanted us to live with them, but I had been firm. As long as we were financially able to do so, I wanted my sister and brother to grow up in their own home and know they had that much security. Mrs. Findley insisted that we call her Aunt Cathy and she took my side. I tried hard to be a parent as well as a big brother, especially to Mikey.

He needed love with a very firm hand, and he did feel comfortable with our relationship. In reality, I guess I did spoil him to a certain extent.

I attended the local college so that I could be at home. I had to smile as I remembered how mortified I felt when Mikey had burst into my Latin class and yelled out in front of the teacher and the class. "Hey, Andy. I just found out where baby ears of corn come from. The stalk brings them." Laughing wildly he ran back to join his class for the special musical that was being held in our building.

That same year he had been a trial and a tribulation to me. Everyone knew how much I loved anything with pumpkin in it. Susan and Aunt Cathy had baked two pumpkin pies and three dozen pumpkin cookies. One pie disappeared, and naturally, I was suspect.

Mikey, with a wicked grin, reminded us that he had told us he was going to the park to play ball. He never denied taking the pie, just skirted the issue. I had always made allowances for him, but this time I was angry. I was working on an assignment, but wrote, "My brother, Mikey, has a dimple in his chin which is matched by a devilish grin. He was clever and sly when he stole a pie and I was blamed for his sin." Poor prose, but it expressed my indignation. I laid the paper down and forgot about it.

Susan was dusting and found the poem. She illustrated it showing Mikey with horns sprouting from his forehead and tiptoeing away holding a steaming pie. She showed me in a lounge chair in another room with a halo over my head. She and Aunt Cathy were shown in the kitchen sweating over a hot stove.

When she showed this to me, I had to laugh. It was clever and very well done. Mikey was delighted and stole it to show to Mrs. Carson, Susan's homeroom teacher. Mrs. Carson was impressed with Susan's art work, and showed it to Mr. Forbes, head of the Art Department. He looked through Susan's work folder and selected three additional sketches and entered them in a state competition. Susan's work won and she was awarded a scholarship for college.

My memories began to tumble rapidly through my head. Mikey breezed through high school, an excellent student, a football hero and winner of Science awards. Mr. Popularity and many other titles were given to him. Although we were forever having to bail him out of small troubles, he never did anything to being disgrace to the family.

I finished at the University of Virginia and surprised everyone, me included, by becoming a doctor instead of going into music. My life has been good. I have a good marriage and great children. I had said I wasn't sure I wanted children after raising Mikey, but I love them dearly and used my experience with Mikey to work with them.

Susan finished college and went to Paris for two years to study art. She is now working in television advertising and is also an interior decorator.

Mikey was in ROTC through high school and majored in science studies in college. He entered the Army Air Force as a first Lieutenant and became an astronaut. My darling, little, mischievous, annoying, lovable, clownish brother was now a valuable person in top secret government work. Who would have expected it? He hadn't married although I told him I could hardly wait for him to have children of his own that would act just as he had.

Then the horror! A plane hijacked and U.S. citizens, as well as people from other countries, were being held hostage in Beirut. Many days were spent in prayer and tears. Every church held special prayer services, printing a list of all the hostages.

A few of the captured people were released. They all spoke highly with love and respect for Colonel Michael Rutherford. Mikey had kept everyone's spirits up with inspiring talks, prayer, Bible stories and favorite verses. Mikey had matured at last. Twenty-eight years old and David Michael Rutherford was a hero. A dead hero.

Looking up at the beautifully stained glass windows, a ray of sunshine seemed to be dancing there. *Dear God, thank you for sharing Mikey with us even for such a short time. He is your ray of sunshine, but he meant so much to us while we had him. I guess he had accomplished all that he was placed on Earth to do. He's now with mother and dad and most important, I know he's with you, Lord.*

I looked to my left and smiled at my precious wife, Holly. On her left were our ten-year-old twins, Michael and Granville and three year old Benjamin. On my right were Susan and her husband, Dr. Richard Mullins and their three year old daughter, Amelia. Susan was expecting another child soon.

My thoughts came back to the present when I heard the minister say, "For everything there is an appointed time. A time to give birth and a time to die" (Ecclesiastes 3, 1-8).

I was going to remind everyone to tell those we love that we do love them before it's too late to tell them. Have compliments and something nice to say to people and leave them with good feelings and good memories.

Holly and I made a pact when we were married that we would never go to bed angry at each other. I added, never leave the house in anger because I could not get over letting my father leave knowing I was angry at him, and he was killed before I could tell him that I really loved him.

Time would help with the grief in our hearts. We would never forget, it would just get a little easier. I won't say good-bye my darling little brother because it is too permanent. I'll just say so long and know we'll be together some day.

THE DEATH OF JIM DAVIS

Jim Davis was dead. Or at least he thought he was dead. The world around him was black as could be and he couldn't feel anything. He wondered how and why he had died. *I really wasn't ready to go yet, but I know we don't have a say in what happens to us. No one wants to die, but at least, I'm ready. I know where my soul is. Am I a ghost? Or is this my soul feeling all of this?*

Too bad he couldn't talk to his employees at the Davis Insurance and Real Estate Agency. If you had ask any of his employees, each one would have said he was arrogant in business, manipulative in that he never gave up, but he was an excellent businessman and they admired him. That was the main reason they were willing to work for him. He ran a tight, but honest ship. He drove himself relentlessly and expected the same of all employees. He was like the old saying, "give a duck a dry rock and in a short time, it will have a small pool of water."

Jim had a talent for making anything he tried work. He carefully planned each of his efforts and thought through everything carefully, plotting the pros and cons of each. He investigated every possible client. He was often called upon to speak at various groups to share how he had achieved so much when he had a heartbreaking start in life.

His employees were loyal and true because, he not only paid well but he was fair and loyal to them.

Jim's father had been in the Marines and, while in England, had met a beautiful, young, hard-working country girl, Hannah Walker. They were married and he brought her back home to Raleigh, North Carolina where he took over his father's business building and repairing cars and some farm machinery.

Hannah loved her husband and tried desperately to be a good wife and homemaker, but she couldn't shake her feeling of home-sickness. Jim realized this and paid for her to go back to England for her parent's thirtieth wedding anniversary. She hated to return to the United States, but loved her husband. She was soon very happy because after one and one half years of marriage she was expecting their first child.

The baby was a healthy boy with a set of powerful lungs. He was nine pounds and ten ounces, a big baby for such a small woman. Hannah's heart overflowed with love and contentment. Her husband and her precious baby were all she wanted in her world.

James Allen Davis, Junior grew to be a rambunctious, athletic young man with a keen desire to learn all he could about everything around him. He was a high school football hero although he never had best buddies or anyone too close. He was pleasant and likeable, but he didn't seem to care about having a group of friends. He was what's known as a loner.

In his third year of high school, his mother died after having struggled for more than a year with cancer of the pancreas. He grieved because he had idolized his mother and her sweet, calm encouraging manner. His father seemed to lose heart when he lost his wife whom he adored. He loved his son but his wife had been his heart.

Jim was not interested in taking over his father's business. Jim, Sr. had planned well for retirement and had a small, but comfortable, income. The home was paid for, so he had no worries about shelter. He sold the business and banked the money for Jim's college education.

Jim took college in stride, learning quickly and making top grades as easily as he had all through his education experiences. He had a phenomenal memory and retained easily. Some of his instructors encouraged him to consider politics, but he was not interested.

In his last semester of college, his father quietly went to sleep and didn't wake. Jim always thought his father had grieved for his mother until his heart could take no more.

Jim sold the family house and put his business sense to work. His father had taught him well -- to work hard, treat people fairly, push himself and expect great things. He also taught his son to face adversities and put them to work for him.

An old friend of his father's owned an insurance and real estate agency. Anthony Quarrels offered Jim a position in his office. Jim eagerly learned all he could and actually built the business for Mr. Quarrels. When Mr. Quarrels, a widower with no children, died, Jim was surprised and appreciative to find that Mr. Quarrels had deeded the business to him.

Jim filed all legal papers and changed the name to Davis Insurance and Real Estate Agency. He retained the office staff because he felt they knew the business and would work well. They did work well together and, again because of

Jim's drive and fairness, the business increased and additional staff had to be employed.

Other business people often resented Jim because he was a veritable bull when he proceeded with his plans. He purchased valuable land on the edge of town that many other had wanted. Jim had homes, a school and a strip mall built which prospered and made him even richer.

Jim was quick to respond to the needs of others and he often helped and encouraged young people. Much to the chagrin of several influential citizens, Jim bought more property, that several had tried to gain, and donated it to the county with the understanding that it would have a stable of horses, a ball field and a teen recreation building. Young people who were from families who could not afford much or young people who were in minor trouble, were encouraged to benefit form these offerings.

Jim hired an expert horse trainer and good instructors with the knowledge that they would be working with children who were angry or hurt and needed to be trusted with animals to build their self-confidence. He also hired well-trained adults to work with the young people in sports and in activities held in the recreation building.

It didn't faze him that some people prophesied he was only getting a group of "bad" children together who would learn from each other and put the townspeople in danger of their lives. He was so thankful for his blessings, he was willing and eager to share. It never failed to surprise people how he prospered and continued to do well.

Spiritual leaders used him as an example of "cast your bread (money and talents) on the water and it will be returned three fold to you"

A lot of people felt uncertain around him because he didn't gather friends around. He didn't attempt to build a big social standing. He was satisfied with his own company. These people were suspicious of his behavior and gossiped about what he was doing privately. Truthfully they were jealous.

At the age of thirty, Jim married a twenty-four year old woman, Joylyn Cahn, who had worked briefly for him. He felt they were equals and that she would be an asset to him. He loved her in his own way, but he was not demonstrative. He did love children and hoped for his own. At first Joylyn was pleased to be the wife of a wealthy man who was so well known that he was recognized in several national papers.

Joylyn became a socialite who attended all the occasions that would bring recognition first to her and to her husband's business. Secretly she had birth control pills because she didn't want to give up any of the social whirl or have, as she explained, her figure ruined with pregnancy. Jim wondered they had no children, but thought it would happen in the right time.

When a couple of years passed with no signs of a baby, Jim suggested that they adopt. Joylyn pretended to agree with him, but always had other plans or made arrangements for Jim to be occupied with something that would prevent him from applying for a child.

During the following year Jim went to their doctor for his annual physical check-up. As he was leaving one of the nurses ran after him saying, "Mrs. Davis left this behind when she was here last week. I know she needs it."

Jim thanked her and when he got to his car he sat in the car and checked to see what the nurse had given him. He was appalled to discover the birth control pill prescription. He didn't want to face the fact that his wife had lied to him and had not been as honest as he thought she was. He drove around aimlessly trying to think of the best way to approach her with this shocking news. He finally went to the teen recreation building to have something in his mind that he enjoyed thinking about.

After dinner that night Jim again talked of adopting children. He looked lovingly at his wife. "I know you're as sorry as I am that we haven't had children of our own. Why don't we go together to our doctor and be tested to see if there's a possibility we can be helped in some way. There's always vitro fertilization."

"What!" Joylyn almost yelled. "Are you crazy? I refuse to put myself through that. Besides, it would be too expensive and you can use the money for children who need it." She tried to flirt with him and change the subject.

"Don't you want children?" Jim asked.

"Well," she answered slowly, "maybe some day, but we need to do more for ourselves first. When we have children I want to be an at home mother and give them all the advantages that children deserve."

He took the package out of his pocket still smiling at her. "Then why have you been on these all our married life and lied to me about it?"

Joylyn took the package and paled when she saw what it was.

"Where did you get this?" she asked angrily.

"Nurse Anne Copely thought she was doing you a favor because you left it behind when you were in the office a few days ago. She gave it to me and explained that you had been on them for a few years. She had no idea that I wasn't aware of your duplicity. I thought all of this time that you were honest with me. I guess this proves you haven't loved me as much as I've loved you."

"Oh, but I do love you," she exclaimed, jumping up to sit on his lap. He stood quickly and walked out of the room. She followed him pleading and trying to give her reasons for using birth control.

Jim didn't answer her. He quietly went into one of the guest bedrooms and gently closed the door. He didn't respond to her entreaties and spent the night alone in the guest bedroom.

The next morning he quietly showered, dressed and left the house to have breakfast in a hotel restaurant, and then went on to work. Being a man who kept his private life just that -- private, he didn't speak of his home troubles with anyone. As far as his staff knew, he was happily married. None of the staff had liked Joylyn when she worked a few months with them, but they said nothing about her to Jim.

One staff member knew better. He had seen Joylyn with a local attorney several times in locations that were certainly not business. He realized that Jim's wife was not faithful.

Jim went on as usual, working, going home and sleeping in the guest room. He was not, and never had been, a violent man, therefore, he took his time deciding what he should do.

Joylyn, though, had told her attorney friend that she was afraid she would be divorced and end with nothing. She had loved living with Jim's money and his great reputation. The attorney, Quentin Elam, was from one of the most prominent families in the city and feared that his reputation might be ruined in the event Jim Davis ask for a divorce and named him as correspondent. Too, he didn't know whether Jim had hired a detective to follow Joylyn and gain evidence. If so, it would surely involve Quentin. He made arrangements of his own to protect himself.

A couple of days later Jim, went to a nearby city to look at some property he was considering purchasing. He was walking down an unfamiliar street after dark because the real estate agent could not meet him any sooner to show him the building. As he passed an alley he saw, out of the corner of his eye, the shadow forms of more than one man walking out of the alley.

Suddenly he felt an arm around his neck and knew he was being pulled into the alley where other people could not see him. He was a strong man who worked out in a gym several times a week and was a brown belt in Shotokon karate. Jim fought valiantly but found that three men were beating and kicking him. He realized he was out-numbered and it was hopeless to fight.

Malodorous odors told Jim he was lying in filth of rotting food and other forms of trash. He couldn't see because one eye was swollen completely shut and the other one hurt too much to try to open. He hurt all over and realized several bones were broken.

Everything went black. He didn't know how long he had lain there against the cold, filthy, broken concrete and pebbles and dirt. A loud noise brought him around when a truck pulled in the alley to empty the dumpster which Jim was lying half under. He wasn't sure whether he was alive or dead. He needed to let the men know before they ran over him.

He couldn't move or make a sound. He couldn't even whisper. He did something he hadn't done since he was a small child at his beloved mother's knees. Even though he knew nothing else, he knew to pray.

"Hey! Look here." One man jumped off the truck while the driver stopped the truck to see who was lying in the alley.

"Man, this poor sap has been worked over but good. Wonder who he is."

By now the driver was kneeling by Jim. "He's barely breathing. I can't find any identification. No wallet, no watch, nothing. Even his shoes are gone. We better get the fuzz here and let them call an ambulance."

Jim was too weak to talk, therefore, no one knew whom they had picked up in the alley. He was taken to Community Hospital, more dead than alive, instead of the big Piedmont Hospital. Community would take patients who couldn't afford to pay much -- if anything.

The police tried desperately to identify him, but faced a stone wall. Even the tags had been ripped from his clothing. The police wanted to keep as much information as they could quiet hoping that someone would start talking and give themselves away.

A week went by and Joylyn filled a missing person's report. Quentin told her to be patient that Jim might have gotten angry and left the area. He told her to withdraw money from the bank and put it in another bank in her name alone. He encouraged her to bring him deeds to the house, the car, etcetera and he would put everything in her name to protect her. She wondered what she needed to be protected from, but was enamored of Quentin.

Joylyn was only too glad to let Quentin take control as long as she could have money and spend it as she wished. She had no interest in the business. Quentin advised her to tell the manager to take charge until further notice.

Robert Morris, the one who had seen Joylyn with Quentin, wondered if he should share this information. He agonized over it for a couple of days and finally asked to have a private conference with the manager, Charles Boggs.

Charles was distressed and decided that they should talk to the attorneys for the business. He and Robert went one afternoon for an appointment with Pernell, Ashburn and Stratton.

Bruce Pernell was alarmed. "How long have you known about Mrs. Davis seeing the other man?"

Robert looked uncomfortable. "I first saw them having dinner at the Gourmet Delight about two months ago, but thought nothing about it. Later I saw them cuddled in a car. I kept seeing them even in the next town of Oakton and realized that this was not a casual friendship. She was crawling all over him."

Pernell was angry. I wish we'd known about this earlier. It's been over a week and no one has seen, or heard from, Jim Davis. I smell a very disagreeable odor."

Anthony Straton was looking thoughtful and listening carefully to all that was said. "Gentlemen, I suggest we hire a detective to investigate the actions of Mrs. Davis and do all that can be done to find Mr. Davis."

"Please keep this conversation in this room with the five of us. The fewer that know of it, the better chance we'll have of finding the truth," Bruce Ashburn said. The men agreed, shook hands and went their own way.

"Robert, the first thing we have to do is put a stop to Mrs. Davis taking any more money from company accounts. I'll tell her we're having an audit of the books since we don't know where Mr. Davis is," Charles decided.

Charles and Robert went to the SunTrust Bank about fifteen minutes before closing on that day. Charles explained that a stop was to be made on company accounts until an audit could be made because of the disappearance of Mr. Davis. He had been given written authority to do this as soon as the company organized.

"But Charles, in the meantime we need money to operate on," Robert worried.

"Jim has a special account in the Mercantile Bank for emergencies such as this. Don't tell anyone about it. In the meantime, it's business as usual,"

Charles called the staff together and explained that business would go on as usual until Mr. Davis could be found. Charles, Jim and the secretary, Meredith Manor, were authorized to sign checks. Two signatures were required, so Charles and Merry would sign checks. The staff was worried about Mr. Davis. It wasn't like him to disappear without telling them he would be gone.

Two days later Joylyn came storming into the office demanding to be told why she could not get money from the bank.

"Mrs. Davis, that's a business account and since Mr. Davis has been absent over a week, the attorneys are conducting an audit of the financial books. None of us can get anything from that account. Don't you and Mr. Davis have a personal account?" Charles asked.

"What of it? If it's any of your business, I've used up all that money. There was none placed in the account last Friday as Jim usually does."

"I'm sorry, Mrs. Davis. Maybe you can talk to our attorneys and they'll explain it better to you. By the way, are you aware that Mr. Davis has placed ownership of all his property in company hands?"

"What! Does that mean I can't sell the car or house or anything to get money?"

"I'm afraid that's true."

She stood and stared at Charles with an icy, evil glare, her face getting redder by the second with her temper. She put an arm out to sweep the computer off his desk, but Charles quickly put his hand on the computer so that she couldn't destroy it. She gave a strangled scream and kicked his wastebasket across the floor. Picking up a heavy stapler, she threw it through a front plate-glass window. Everyone hurried to get between her and anything she could destroy. Screaming obscenities, she stamped out of the office slamming the door behind her.

"What brought that on?" Susan Kerns ask bewildered.

"I suspect she's been stripping the business account for some time," Robert explained. "Jim Davis is a great guy. He would not disappear like this by his own volition. We'll just have to pray and hope he'll turn up soon, or at least news of him."

In the hospital, Jim was hurting too much to think about anything. At first he was kept sedated. As days went by, and he gained strength, he was only given pain medication as needed. He could not remember who he was or what had happened to him. It was confusing and upsetting.

"I feel as if I work among several people, but I can't remember. Am I married? Do I have children?"

The doctors tried to keep Jim from worrying. Dr. Mark Gentry smiled at him. "I think you are married, or at least you were. There is a line on your ring finger showing there was once a ring there. Maybe it was taken from you when you were beaten. Try not to get upset or think too hard. Please relax, be patient and it'll come to you in good time when your mind is ready for it.

"Tell me how I can keep from worrying. What's going on that I might be a part of? If I have a family, they must be in shock and worrying about where I am. How long have I been here?"

"Three weeks. You still have some healing to do. We'll help all we can and the police are trying to find if someone has ask about you."

The Clearmont Police finally received notice of a missing person and thought the description might match the unknown man in the hospital. Lt. Dave Garrison called the phone number on the poster and was answered by Joylyn.

"Ma'am, my name is Lt. Garrison of the Clearmont Police. I have a notice that you're searching for a missing husband. Is this description of the poster accurate?"

"Of course it is. Why would I search for my husband and not give his description? Do you have someone who matches the poster or are you just wasting my time?"

He was accustomed to all kinds of personalities, and paid no attention to her rude behavior. "I'll apologize if I'm calling at a bad time, but if this is your husband, he's in Community Hospital here in Clearmont."

"I'll get over there some time today and check for myself." She hung up without thanking him or conversing further.

Lt. Garrison wrote all of this on a report making a comment that he was suspicious of her attitude.

Joylyn wasted no time in picking up the phone and calling Quentin. "I was hoping he had disappeared for good. What do you think happened to him?" She listened impatiently for a moment. "Well, they're expecting me over there to see for myself. Will you go with me?"

"No! I must not be seen with you. We don't want people talking and thinking the wrong things. Now do we? Why don't you go check and let me know."

"I have no money and I need gas for my car. I'll need to eat also and I might have to stay over. You'll need to give me some money. Five hundred should be enough."

"Five hundred! Are you crazy? I can't give you that much money. In fact, it's time you forget you ever knew me. Don't call me any more. You've conveniently forgotten that I'm married and have two children. I can't afford to get mixed up in something that would hurt my reputation or my marriage." He slammed the phone down.

Joylyn smirked and sashayed across the room talking aloud. She flipped her hair up off the back of her neck. "Well, big boy. So you bail out at the first hint of something unpleasant. We'll see about that." Joylyn spoke sarcastically as she lit a cigarette and went out to sit by the side of the swimming pool and plan.

She smoked and thought, frowning and cursing to herself. She finally went in and dressed in a swim suit. Coming out she ran toward the pool and dived in. Furiously she swam from one length to the other several times and crawled out breathless.

Joylyn walked as if she were stamping ants as she went back into the house, showered, dressed and ran out to her car. She had found some bills in a coat pocket of Jim's. Thirty dollars wouldn't get her far, but it would do right now. She smirked and giggled to herself thinking of how she was going to approach Quentin's wife and talk to her.

Reaching the hospital late in the afternoon, she went in and stood at the desk in the lobby.

"Good afternoon. May I help you?" The white-haired, friendly lady inquired.

"Yeah, I guess you can. I think my missing husband is here. Some Garrison fellow called me from the police and said a man was here that had not been identified. Could I see him?"

"Oh, my goodness. I hope it is your missing husband. Please have a seat and I'll call someone to take you up to his room."

"Well, hurry it up. I haven't got all day." Joylyn sailed over and sat in the lobby, arranging her legs and skirt to her best advantage.

In just over five minutes a nurse came and stood before her. "Hello. I'm Helen Wheatley. If you'll come with me I'll take you to see the unknown man. I hope it is your husband." The nurse didn't mention she'd also notified the police.

"I don't care what your name is and I don't really care if it is my husband. He's been gone almost a month."

Helen looked at the receptionist and raised her eyebrows. Smiling she escorted Joylyn to the elevator. "It's a lovely day, isn't it? The flowers in our garden are appreciating the sun after the light rain last night. Maybe you'd like to view our garden at the east side of the building."

"I didn't come to look at flowers or to have conversation with the hired help. Just get me to the room." Joylyn was working her face into such ugly lines that the nurse privately hoped the nice man didn't belong to this woman.

The nurse led Joylyn to the fourth floor and stood before room number four sixteen. Joylyn brushed by her and threw the door open. She stamped over to the bed and looked down at the patient.

Jim was puzzled. *Who is this woman and why does she seem so angry?*

"There you are. Thought you could hide from me, didn't you? Well, you won't get away with it." Joylyn screeched.

The nurse gently pulled her back from the bed. "This man has amnesia and has been very sick. He almost died from a severe beating and was left in an alley for dead."

Joylyn gave a harsh laugh and turned toward Jim. "You always land on your feet, don't you? I've never seen anyone with such luck. Well, say something." Joylyn ordered Jim angrily.

"Ma'am, I'm sorry, but I don't know you and have no idea what you're talking about." Jim spoke patiently.

While Joylyn was yelling and being abrasive with Jim, the floor nurse had called for the doctor who had been working with Jim. Dr. Conrad Dawson was in his late thirties and very handsome. He was five-eleven and worked out in the gym as often as he could. He had wavy, black hair and the bluest eyes. All the nurses swooned when he passed them.

Dr. Dawson came into the room and took in the situation at a glance. His first reaction was sympathy with the patient. "Hello. I'm Dr. Dawson and this is my patient. Do you recognize him?"

"Sure I do. He's my husband, Jim Davis, and he has an insurance and real estate office in Stone Gap. Why won't he talk to me?"

"Mrs. Davis, this is a very sick man. He was at death's door when he was found and brought to us. He doesn't know who he is or what happened to him. He doesn't remember about his life. If you would be so kind, will you come to my office and give me the necessary information about him?"

As he was talking, Lt. Garrison slid quietly in the room. Two of the nurses had already told him of Mrs. Davis' actions.

Joylyn turned and got a good look at the doctor. She immediately had a gleam of a predator in her eyes and snuggled up to him. "Sure, I'll go with you. Just tell me what you want."

"Now Mrs. Davis, I imagine you want to know about your husband's condition before you give us the information we need."

"Yeah. Yeah. I see the old fuddy-duddy is sick. What happened to him and why doesn't he remember anything?"

Lt. Garrison entered the office and thanked Dr. Dawson for having him called. "The gentleman was beaten severely and left in an alley for dead. Blows to his head caused the brain to be traumatized and, as a result, he lost his memory. Hopefully as he gains strength, he'll remember."

Joylyn made a face and looked at the doctor. "Can he sign papers and checks now? I need money. You know, to pay bills, get gas for my car and etcetera.

"No, I'm sorry. He cannot be bothered with any business of any kind. It would not be legal to have him sign anything until he is aware of what he is doing." He turned to the policeman.

"Lt. Garrison, this is Mrs. Davis. She's established that our unknown man is her husband, Mr. Jim Davis of Stone Gap where they live and he has a business. We still don't know what he was doing here in Clearmont or what, or rather who, happened to him."

Lt. Garrison spoke gently to Joylyn although he had formed an opinion of her that he didn't like. "I'm sorry, Mrs. Davis, that you have to be disturbed, but I'm relieved to know who the patient is. When was the last time you saw your husband?"

"Well, I AM disturbed. I have other important things that I need to do today. Let's get this over with so I can be on my way."

Dr. Dawson and Lt. Garrison looked at each other in astonishment. Lt Garrison just smiled and continued talking. "When was the last time you saw your husband?"

"Let's see, this is Wednesday the twenty-third, so I guess it was the twenty-first of last month. Yeah, that's it."

"Did he say where he was going or who he had to meet?" Lt. Garrison asked.

"No. the idiot was mad at me, so he had been sleeping in one of our guest bedrooms. He got up and left before I did, so I had no idea where he was going or who he was meeting. I just know the stupid manager of his business closed all bank accounts and called for an audit of the books because he had disappeared."

"Why was he angry with you?' Lt. Garrison questioned.

"That's private business and I don't have to answer that. He was just real mad, but he won't fight fair. When he's angry, he goes off by himself and won't quarrel or get it out of his system like I do." She smiled seductively at both men.

"Mrs. Davis, you'll have to come down to the station and fill out some papers and I'm sure the hospital will need information from you. Does Mr. Davis have medical insurance?"

"Of course he does, but I think you should find who did this to him and make them pay. And make them pay me, too, for having to do without my husband."

"But you said you hadn't shared a room for some time." Dr. Dawson reminded her.

"I meant I need the money that he would have been giving me. Quentin says --" She stopped with a thoughtful gleam in her eyes.

"Who's Quentin?" Lt. Garrison asked nonchalantly but with an alert mind.

"Oh, Quentin Elam. He's an attorney and a very good friend of mine. He'll advise me what to do," she said smugly.

Lady I wonder if you and this Quentin had something to do with Mr. Davis' beating. Lt. Garrison's mind was racing.

"We've already notified the Police Department in Stone Gap that we have the missing person. They'll also be in touch with you."

"Well, for heaven's sake," she yelled. "Can't all of you just let me alone and see to it that Jim signs checks for me?"

Lt. Garrison shook his head and stood. He glared down at her from his six-two height, his deep grey eyes showing that he read her like a book. His sandy hair was cut short in police regulation. She tried flirting, but he wasn't interested.

"I'll leave Mrs. Davis with you, Dr. Dawson, and good luck." Lt. Garrison added as he strode from the room.

"What a rude man," Joylyn fumed. "Well, where are the papers you want me to fill out. I guess I'll have to go to the police station as long as I'm here. Where are the papers? I haven't got all day."

Lt. Garrison was furious as he drove back to the station. He felt sorry for Jim Davis and understood why he had not occupied a bedroom with his wife. "Poor sucker. Probably led a dog's sorry life." he mused.

In the station he found Detective Jerry Stone waiting to talk to him. "The manager of Davis Insurance and Real Estate hired me to find Mr. Davis and also to find whatever I could on Mrs. Davis. I found she is having an affair with an attorney by the name of Quentin Elam who is a married man with a family. I have no proof, but my guess would be that they hoped to have Mr. Davis killed and have a clear path to money and their brand of pleasure."

Lt. Garrison leaned back in his chair and made a teepee of his hands in front of him. "I was suspicious of Mr. Elam when Mrs. Davis kept mentioning him. There was a sparkle in her eyes when she talked of him. Keep this quiet for a while and I want to lay a little trap of my own."

"What kind of trap and may I help?" the detective asked.

"Mrs. Davis will be tied up for a short time filling out papers. When she comes to the station, I'm going to tell one of the officers to make sure he keeps her as long as he can. In the meantime, I want to go to Stone Gap and talk to the Police Chief there. It's out of my jurisdiction, but I'm hoping he'll cooperate with my plans."

"I know Chief Burrows and he's an all right guy." Jerry nodded.

"Let's go then and I'll tell the Chief about my plan at the same time I tell you."

Twenty minutes later, Lt. Garrison and Detective Stone pulled in front of the Stone Gap Police Department building. Chief Burrows was glad to see them. They told the Chief what they had found about the disappearance of Jim Davis and outlined the plan. The Chief was more than willing to cooperate, in fact, he went with them to visit Attorney Elam.

The three men gave their names to the secretary and told her it was imperative that they speak with Attorney Elam immediately. She went back to Quentin's office and came back inviting them to follow her to a conference room. "Would you like something to drink? We have tea, coffee and soft drinks."

"Thank you, but no. We'll only be here a few minutes," Chief Burrows smiled at her.

Quentin Elam came strutting and bouncing into the room. "Gentlemen! To what do I owe this honor?"

"Mr. Elam," Chief Burrows started, "this is Lt. Garrison from the Clearmont Police Department and Detective Stone from here in Stone Gap. We need to discuss something of utmost important with you -- privately," he added as he looked at the secretary.

"Miss Curry, thank you. It's all right. You may go back to your desk," Quentin told the lady.

"Now, how can I be of assistance to you gentlemen?" Quentin clasped his hands behind his head, looking as if they were privileged to be in his presence.

"We want the truth," Chief Burrows answered.

"Well, of course, the truth. I'm an officer of the court and must tell the truth," Quentin grinned. Looking at the stern expressions on the men's faces, his grin faded and he sat up straight.

"Detective Stone, you start by telling him why you're here," Chief Burrows instructed.

"I was sent by the officers of the Davis Insurance and Real Estate Agency to follow Mrs. Davis and report to them." He then read from his notes his written report of the dates, times and places where he had observed Quentin and Joylyn. "Going to the Harvest Motel was not a good idea because so many people go there for nefarious purposes."

"How dare you," Quentin said quietly through gritted teeth. "How dare you follow me and report my activities."

"He was following Mrs. Davis and you were with her. If you were doing honest activities, there would be no need for you to complain or be worried," Lt. Garrison told him.

"Who's worried? I've done nothing to be ashamed of."

"Not according to Mrs. Davis," Lt. Garrison sat on the edge of his chair looking straight in Quentin's eyes. "She told us quite a bit about you this afternoon."

Quentin jumped up and started pacing. "She's a liar. I had dinner with her a couple of times because she needed advise about her marriage. And that's all," Quentin said leaning over to speak directly to Lt. Garrison.

Detective Stone smiled. "And that advice included four complete nights in a motel?" Again he read the dates.

Quentin wilted and sunk into his chair. "Oh, Lord. I'm sunk when my wife gets word of this."

"She's not the only one you need to worry about. I know you wouldn't dirty your own hands, but who did you hire to beat Jim Davis in hopes of killing him?" Lt. Garrison spat out.

"That was Joylyn's idea. She said if he were dead, she could take the money and liquidate all holdings and have a lot to live on. She threatened to talk with my wife if I didn't help her."

"You're each blaming the other. Who did you hire? They left the poor man beaten and broken. He probably would have been better off dead, but he's going to be great." Chief Burrows added.

Quentin reluctantly gave the information they wanted. Chief Burrows called a group of officers in and told them to go find the men that Quentin named. He told two of the officers to take Quentin and charge him with attempted murder.

Joylyn was shocked when she returned home and found Chief Burrows, Lt. Garrison and Detective Stone waiting for her. She screamed bloody murder when they told her what they were charging her with. She, of course, said it was all Quentin's idea. Chief Burrows had two officers ready to take her to the station and charge her. "Don't let her and Mr. Elam get together or talk at all."

Roger and Charles were ecstatic. They felt free to tell the staff what they had been investigating and what had happened to Jim Davis. Everyone was overjoyed that he had been found but was disturbed at his condition.

Two months after he had disappeared, Jim Davis was healing and getting his memory back. He was grateful for his loyal employees and gave a generous bonus in their

Christmas paycheck. Needless to say, he had a divorce from Joylyn and she had nothing.

He was sorry for Mrs. Elam. She had two teenagers to think about. Jim offered to look into Quentin's dealings and help set up a trust fund for the children. He, without her knowledge, placed some of his own money in the account. Quentin's two partners kept the business going and sent Mrs. Elam a modest check each month.

Jim never remarried and worked until he couldn't physically do anything. He retired with a good income that he was well prepared for and sold the business to two of the men who had worked well with him.

At the age of eighty-nine, Jim went peacefully to sleep. He had not been a church going man, but he did have faith and believed. Everyone admired him, but followed his wishes and had a celebration of life instead of a funeral. Now Jim Davis was finally at rest. Now the death of Jim Davis was a fact.

THE HEART OF GREY WARRIOR

The year of nineteen thirty-two saw a majority of the people in grave financial trouble. The Rutherford ranch was no exception. Mason Leigh Rutherford had a fifteen thousand acre ranch in Texas where he raised some of the best horses in the United States. It took a great deal of money to operate a ranch of that size. (Tools, machinery, fencing, feed, farrier, veterinarian, food for people and items people needed for personal use.)

Mason and Mary Rutherford had five living sons. Two daughters and a son had died either at birth or soon after. Mason had given each of his sons a section of land, and, as each boy grew and married, he built a home and barns on his land, but continued to work for his father at the main ranch.

One of the last horses Mason trained was an iron grey stallion, Thoroughbred and Quarter cross. He was long-legged with powerful shoulders and rump. Mason hoped the grey would sire many valuable horses for him. There was something extra special about this horse. He formed an attachment for Mason that made him seem almost human. In fact, he followed Mason around like a puppy because Mason had handled him from the day he was foaled and had trained him.

On Mason's eighty-sixth birthday, he had to admit that he could not see as well as he had and not well enough to work by himself. This was a blow to his ego. His sight gradually left him, but he was too proud to give up.

One fall day, when the boys were out working on the range, Mason became restless. While Mary was busy in the kitchen, he slowly made his way to the main barn. Walking quietly by the farrier's shop, he could hear men talking as they worked. He was careful to not call attention to himself. Feeling his way around the tack room, he took his familiar bridle and saddle down. He brushed and saddled Grey Warrior and carefully mounted.

"It's up to you, boy. I need your eyes and you know the land. Let's go for a ride." Mason let the horse head in a direction he knew and let him have his head.

Everyone came in early when the great thunderheads rolled in from the west. By the time the men were in, cold rain was coming down in sheets. The lightning bounced around as if it were being hurtled through the sky from Zeus' hammer.

Mary called out to her oldest son as he rode by going to his house.

"Franklin, have you seen your daddy? I can't find him anywhere."

"No, Mom. I haven't. What in the world is he doing out?" he ask sharply. "I'm tired and wet and want to get home, but I'll look for him." he didn't want to worry his mother by saying that he hoped his dad was not injured and lying in the cold rain.

Franklin turned his horse and rode to the barn. "Hey, Ben," he called to his youngest brother. "Is dad in the barn with you?"

"No. I haven't seen him since this morning," Ben replied as he forked fresh hay to the horses.

Franklin whirled his tired horse and ran to the house, jumped off and ran up the step to the porch. He grabbed the rope and rang the big brass bell that was used to call people together in an emergency. It was not long until all the boys, and most of the ranch hands, were at the house.

The boys were trying to comfort their mother when Ben came running toward them. "Dad's saddle and Grey Warrior are gone," he told them excitedly.

The two oldest boys were married and their wives stayed with Mary, keeping her busy preparing food for everyone. Soon the sons and ranch hands were mounted and riding out in the storm to find Mason and his horse.

"I feel like whipping him like he used to whip me," Jason barked in anger. He rode with one of the three groups that were looking for Mason.

Conrad and two ranch hands were riding down by the river where the railroad bridge crossed over the water. It was not a solid bridge. Strong planks were laid about a foot apart and the rails were over them. One of the ranch hands made a strangling noise as he tried to talk but was too frightened to be coherent. They all looked to the other side of the river.

There sat Mason on the Warrior. The river had swollen until it would be life threatening to try to cross, or swim, as Warrior had obviously done to get to the other side. The current was too swift.

Warrior neighed to the men and tossed his head. "Be quiet," Conrad whispered. "Don't call out. Warrior might jump in to swim to us and they'd both be lost."

For a moment they sat in silence, the storm making it impossible to see clearly in the quickly gathering dusk.

Warrior turned sharply and ran up a slight rise to the tracks. One of the Hispanic cowboys fell off his horse, dropped to his knees, made the sign of the cross and began to pray.

Mason realized Warrior would have to get him home because he could not see. He gave the horse a loose rein. Warrior dropped his head until his nose was on the rail like a dog scenting a track. Warrior carefully stepped on the now slick, wet ties and slowly made his way across. Each man found it hard to breathe as they quietly watched. Reaching the other side, Warrior ran down the bank to stand near the group of men. Still none of them made a sound. They were in shock.

Mason did not know they were there. "Let's go home, boy." Warrior gave a little buck as if to say, "Hey, look at me. Look what I did." He loped home with thankful, but angry men following.

Mary came running out in the rain. "Mason Leigh Rutherford. What am I going to do with you? If you **ever** go out alone again, you will not find me at home when you return."

Mason laughed and hugged her. He knew she would not leave him. Hadn't they been married for sixty-three years?

Mason died the next year and Mary followed him in four months. The sons divided the ranch, the cattle and the horses, but remained neighbors and close friends. Some of their children, and grandchildren, eventually sold their share of the property. It is not the huge ranch it was when Mason and Mary settled it in 1873.

Descendents of Grey Warrior can be found today in several states. They are beautiful, sturdy and proud, but I bet none are as dependable and faithful as the Grey Warrior.

The Grey Warrior was a gentle, happy thirty years old in nineteen fifty-nine when he died.

SCREAMING EAGLE

Jarrod Lee Dover paused for breath and laughed aloud. Playing flag ball with his two brothers and their small children always gave him satisfaction. He got what his sister-in-law, Marilyn. called a goofy look in his eyes as he gazed over the huge lawn at the back of his oldest brother, Jacob's, house.

Dad, Herman Dover and mom, Penelope, sat on the wraparound porch and watched their three sons and grandchildren with pride and love. They couldn't have loved biological children more.

When the Dovers had left Florida and traveled to New Mexico to work as missionaries on an Indian reservation, they were appalled at the condition in which they found some families. As they realized that they were not going to have children of their own, they considered adoption.

There were so many children that needed love and care. Three little boys really tore at their hearts. Neither little boy had blood relations that wanted them. They had previously come from broken families. After many months of appeals, tribal hearings and court attendance, the Dovers finally adopted these three boys and gave them names that they would hopefully be proud of.

The oldest boy, ten years old at the time, was given the name of Jacob Paul Dover. The middle boy, seven years old, was given the name of Jarrett Judson Dover and the youngest, five years old, was given the name Jarrod Lee Dover.

Jacob had only a little Indian blood. He had beautiful, curly, blonde hair and eyes of cornflower blue like his mother. He was a happy boy and willing to be the big brother. The middle boy, Jarrett was a half breed. He had dark brown hair and hazel eyes and was forever more in mischief. The youngest, Jarrod, was full blooded, a solemn youngster with black eyes to match the shiny black hair and the copper skin of a full blood Sioux. He learned quickly; was respectful and polite, but seemed to hold himself back while he watched people around him. When he got out, lost to his brothers, or couldn't keep up with them, Jarrod would shut his eyes and scream his frustration.

Because the reservation, and Indians, was all the boys had known, they decided to give themselves Indian names.

Jarrett was emphatic. "I think Jacob should be called 'White Eyes' because he's so fair. Jacob didn't like this so they waited until they thought about it a while.

One day Jarrett accidently knocked down a hornets nest and came running to the house, screeching like a banshee. He didn't get one sting but he was sure red from running in fright. After we decided that he had not been in any danger, Jacob suggested that Jarrett's name should be Running Scared. Jarrett didn't like that either.

They spent several days talking about names. One day Jarrett was poking around in the garage and found a pistol, in a box, on a top shelf, in the garage. There were bullets also, therefore, he loaded the pistol and swaggered out to show his brothers that he could twirl the pistol like he had seen in a western movie. He dropped the pistol and shot himself in the foot. Days later Jacob laughingly suggested that we change Jarrett's name to Sharp Shooter.

A couple of weeks passed and Jarrod became fearful of what the boys would call him. Time passed and he forgot about it. One day Jacob and Jarrett found popsicles in the freezer. They came out into the yard licking them and making happy sounds to tease Jarrod who was furious that he didn't have one. He flew at them screaming and hitting wherever he could. Mom Dover had to separate the boys and take Jarrod inside where he got a popsicle of his own. Only then did he settle down.

The next day Jacob declared, "I know a great name for Jarrod. I think he should be called Screaming Eagle. Because he screams and attacks." Jarrod drew a breath of relief. It could have been worse. *Mine sounds more like an Indian name than theirs. After all, I'm full blooded,* he consoled himself.

The three boys had a wonderful childhood and were blessed to be adopted by two such loving people. Now they're adults and sharing families. Jacob and Jarrett are married but Jarrod, the youngest, is still single.

Jarrod eased out of the game and went up on the porch to sit beside his parents. "I just thought of something," he began.

"What did you think of, son?" Dad Dover asked.

"Remember the pistol that Jarrett found that time and shot his foot? I know you don't care for firearms. Where did you get the pistol and why was it hidden in the garage?"

Herman and Penelope looked at each other. Herman shifted in his chair and finally spoke. "You boys never knew it, but when we were finally granted custody of you three, some of the Indians on the reservation resented it. A big man, by the name of George something, apparently got drunk, and as we were getting in the car ready to leave for Florida, he came at us waving that pistol and shooting in the air. He said if we didn't give you boys back to him, he was going to shoot us. Several men standing nearby helped me subdue George and I threw the pistol in the trunk of my car and forgot about it. When we unpacked, I found it and had all intentions of giving it to the local police, but forgot it and left it in the box in the garage. Who would have thought it would be found by a boy when it was up so high. We should have remembered Jarrett's propensity for mischief. I gave the gun to the police when they came to question me about Jarrett's accident."

Jarrod laughed so loudly that the others came to the porch to find out what was going on. Anna Marie, Jacob's wife, came to the door.

"Are any of you keeping an eye on the grill? Those hamburgers and hot dogs won't turn themselves. They should be done by now."

Jacob's two sons and a daughter and Jarrett's twins, a boy and girl, gathered around declaring that they were starving.

Jarrett's wife, Sylvia, ask the older children to come get the paper plates, napkins and buns. She and Anna Marie carried potato salad, coleslaw and tableware out. Jarrod went in to get pickles, ketchup, diced onions and butter.

"We have cake and ice cream for dessert," Sylvia told them. "We'll bring it out when we're ready for it. Jacob, ask a blessing so we can eat."

After the blessing, the children made a dash to be served. The adults laughed and hugged any child that got within reach.

Jarrod waved a hamburger in the air and sang loudly to the tune of "They'll be coming around the mountain," -- "They'll be going to the stomach one by one." the children thought he was hilarious, but the adults groaned.

"Boy! We gave you the proper name, Screaming Eagle. You sound just like one," Jarrett teased.

After everyone had eaten all they wanted, the group settled on blankets in the shade of the big oak trees. Full stomachs and quiet moments lulled some of the adults into a restful nap. Most of the children, especially the younger ones, had gone to sleep.

Jacob's boys, Jackson, twelve and Job, ten wouldn't admit that they napped, but they were sound asleep. Jennifer, six, was curled up beside her beloved Uncle Jarrod. Jarret's twins, eleven-year-old Roberto and Rebekah, were, as usual up to their old tricks. Like father -- like -- well, you know.

They winked at each other and quietly slipped away to go to a nearby creek. All of the children had been warned to stay away fro the creek unless an adult was with them. There was a real danger of falling in deep water and maybe Cottonmouth snakes which were seen now and then. What they didn't know was that the next ranch had just purchased a new bull for breeding and turned him loose in the pasture. There was a fence around the property on the other side of the creek. Seeing the children, and hearing them laughing and jumping around, the bull wandered down to the fence to look over at them. Roberto waved his arms and yelled at the bull ordering him to go back to his cows.

The bull, a huge, coal-black fellow, decided that the creature was challenging him, so he charged the fence so hard that he came through causing him to stumble and almost fall. The children then made a big mistake. Instead of climbing a close tree, they took off running and yelling for help. This infuriated the bull who charged across the creek and ran after them bellowing and snorting.

The Dover family heard the cries of the children and the three brothers came to their feet running to help the children, not knowing about the bull. Jarrod was in front and saw the bull first. He waved the children on by him and ran at the bull screaming and ordering the bull to go back. Jacob and Jarrett ran to the house with a child each, yelling at their wives and parents to get in the house and call 9-1-1.

Jarrod was able to swing himself on to a low branch of a tree which the bull promptly butted and bellowed a challenge. It seemed forever, but within ten minutes paramedics, the ranch owner who owned the bull and the Dover hired help were turning the bull back toward his own pasture. A woman paramedic deftly threw a rope and caught the bull around his neck. A Dover hired man roped him from the other side and they held the bull between then.

Within twenty minutes the bull was gone and everyone had gone away except the two paramedics. The woman laughingly told Jarrod that he could come down now.

Blushing and stammering, Jarrod dropped to the ground. The children gathered around him proclaiming him a hero.

"Yeah, Screaming Eagle really came through didn't he?" Jacob laughed until he had the hiccups. The name had to be explained to the two paramedics. The woman, Aleana Marie Osage, told them her father was a full blooded Indian. She looked with interest at the six-three Jarrod with copper skin and amazing black eyes.

The next week, Jarrod saw Aleana in town and invited her to have dinner with him. A month passed and the Dover family was overjoyed to know that Jarrod had seemed to find someone that would be suitable for him.

In October, the town was in high spirits to celebrate the marriage of their beloved Sheriff Jarrod Dover to Aleana Marie Osage. Jarrett, now an attorney, teasingly told Aleana that she could call on him if she had trouble with his baby brother.

The following year, in November, a new little Dover came to join the family. As Herman Lee Dover was laid in the arms of his proud grandfather, Jacob and Jarrett slapped Jarrod on the back and said with love and pride, "You did real good, little brother."

Sioux Indian -- Twenty-Third Psalm

I was given this many years ago as one version of the Twenty-third Psalm according to a group of Sioux Indians.

The **Great Father** above a **Shepherd Chief** is. I am **His** and with **Him** I want not. **He** throws out to me a rope and the name of the rope is love. **He** draws me to where the grass is green and soft and the water not dangerous and I eat and lie down and am satisfied. Sometimes my heart is very weak and I fall down, but **He** lifts me up again and draws me onto a good road. **His** name is **Wonderful.** Sometimes, it may be very soon, it may be a long, long time, **He** will draw me into a valley. It is dark there, but I will be afraid not, for it is between those mountains that the **Shepherd Chief** will meet me and the hunger that I have in my heart all through this life will be satisfied.

Sometimes **He** makes the love rope into a whip, but after that **He** gives me a staff to lean on. **He** spreads a meal for me with all kinds of good food. **He** puts **His** hand on my head and all the tired is gone. My bowl **He** fills until it is spilling over the sides. I lie not. What I tell you is true. These roads that are way in front of me will stay with me through this life and after, and then I will go to live in the Big Tepee and sit down with the **Great Shepherd Chief** forever.

LORD, keep Your arm around my shoulders and Your hand over my mouth.

TIES THAT BIND

Her labored breathing could be heard on the still frosty air as if it were a machine grinding faithfully though struggling. She placed a hand to the ache in her side and ran on as hard as her tired, burning legs could carry her. The pain in her stomach was almost too much to bear, but she still ran on.

Faintly, in the distance behind her, she could hear the howling of the dogs as they followed her scent and kept on her trail in spite of all she could do to mislead them. She knew that even if she had about an hour's head start, the dogs would soon catch up.

Why me? I never encouraged him. Her mind ran over what she knew of the man chasing her with the savage hounds. She knew that unless she made it to the river first, the dogs would soon be snapping at her heels. In her fright she imagined the teeth grabbing her from behind and their hot breaths fanning over her slim body.

She dashed on through the forest, dodging around trees and crashing through briars and thick bushes. *Why won't he leave me alone? What have I ever done to him? He doesn't really even know me.*

The man was a decorated war hero, had come home from the Gulf War a spiritually broken human. His shell-shocked brain built up images that he probably couldn't explain, more over, he probably didn't understand them himself.

Elana O'Brien, in her second year of college, lived at home to help her widowed mother, crippled with arthritis, and to care for her eleven year old sister. As she left the college campus, and boarded the bus to go home, she noticed a strange man staring at her as if he were angry at her. At her stop, she got off the bus and started to walk the block and a half to her home. Her heart jumped with dread when she turned to find that same man walking behind her still staring and saying nothing.

At five-three and hardly one hundred ten pounds, she was no match for the six-two, two hundred thirty pound trained military man. Her short, dark curls danced around her face as she walked faster. Her hazel eyes were worried and her small turned-up nose with its few freckles wrinkled at the dirty, musty odor of his clothing as he came up to her.

Megan O' Brien opened the front door to step out and get a better, anxious look down the street. Elana was two hours late. What could have happened? Her two daughters were so good to let the widowed mother know where they were and when they might get home. Finally, nearing midnight, she called the police station to voice her concern. At first the officer who answered tried to tell her that an adult had to be missing more than twenty-four hours before they put out an APB on them. After hearing her story of Elana's college attendance, her excellent grades and her devoted caring for her mother and little sister, the officer promised to send someone to question the bus driver and anyone that could be contacted. Megan O'Brien sat up all night while Janine finally gave in to the sandman and dropped off to sleep in a lounge chair in the parlor.

Her stomach and side hurt so badly that she could hardly keep moving. Even if she had to die, she would not go back to that dirty, smelly shack where the man kept her, saying nothing, just staring at her. There was no need now to wish she had acted differently. When he first grabbed her and dragged her through the woods to an old shack, she was too surprised and frightened to struggle. He hadn't done anything to her except push her down into a creaky chair. When he went to another room to see about the dogs, Elana made a dash for the door and ran as hard as she could. She struggled on thinking that if she could get to the river, her scent would be lost in the water and the dogs couldn't track her.

As she thankfully crossed the cold water, getting wet to her waist, she started up the other bank as fast as her tired body would drag. Hearing noises behind her, she looked back to discover that the dogs were close and had seen her. It wouldn't matter how much water she was in now because the dogs knew where she was.

Crossing the top of the rise, she breathed a prayer of thanksgiving as she saw a town before her. Running down the hill she kept going until her feet hit the concrete sidewalk. She saw that she was at the corner of Washington St. and Cedar Lane. Ahead, and on the other side of the street, was the Bat Wing Bar and Grill. Even though it was after midnight, there seemed to be someone inside. If she could just make it to the door of the Bar and Grill and call for help. Just as her foot stepped up on the curb to cross the narrow street, she heard the click of claws on the concrete behind her and heard the triumphant howl of the dogs.

Janine sat up screaming. "Mum, Mum, why is sister running? Why is she so afraid? I know where sister is."

Sobbing she held an arm across her aching stomach as she told her mother about seeing signs of Washington St. and Cedar Lane. "Sister was running toward the Bat Wing Bar and Grill."

The mother's hands were shaking so badly she tried twice to punch the number of the Sheriff's station. The deputy was skeptical but did promise to send an officer to investigate. The town was only about eight miles away.

An hour and a half later, two deputies delivered Elana safely to her mother and sister. "Ma'am, I would never have believed such a story if I had not been there and helped rescue your daughter. Is your youngest daughter psychic? How did she know where to find her sister?"

The second deputy added, "We never thought Dave Borden was dangerous. We all knew he had problems that occurred when he was in service. He comes to town for supplies, but he never socializes. I don't think I've ever heard him have a conversation with anyone. We didn't know he had six dogs. How did your daughter know that her sister was running for her life and where to find her?"

"By God's mercy. It is the honest love of sister for sister. There is no greater tie that binds than that of true love."

PLANNING PAYS

This is a true story about an ancestor of mine. My great grandfather, Jessee Bolling was born in 1826. He had an older brother, Ezekiel, born in 1815.

Ezekiel married Nancy Carr and they moved about a day's journey by horse and wagon from Ezekiel's parents, Jeremiah and Sally Ward Bolling. After two years of marriage, Ezekiel and Nancy were blessed with twin girls, Molly and Polly. These little girls were the delight of their hearts. Nancy made cute clothes for them and taught them things a woman should know. Ezekiel got pretty ribbons for their hair at the trading post.

They lived in a wilderness area in what is now called Flat Gap, Virginia, in Wise County. There were friendly and unfriendly Indians. There were a few nice people living a few miles away and a few white trash. Nancy almost had a heart attack if those girls got out of her sight and Ezekiel wasn't much better.

Ezekiel was afraid some of the unfriendly Indians or some of the low-life whites would take his precious girls. He and Nancy taught the girls to take care of each other and of their two little brothers, Jedadiah and Hosea.

Ezekiel taught them, that if they were ever taken from their parents, to not be afraid and to talk to Jesus. He also taught them to take their ribbons, or a part of their full petticoats, and tear them into small pieces. If they could, they were to drop these pieces so that Pappa could follow and rescue them. He even had them practice what they would do if this did occur.

The summer the girls were seven, Nancy was inside making candles and Ezekiel was plowing a rocky field with two worn oxen. Nancy heard a strange noise and looked out to see four naked Indians running off with her little girls. She screamed over and over and Ezekiel came running, leaving the poor oxen standing in the field in the heat. He tried to follow with no result.

Nancy was holding the two boys and crying when three strange men came by that had been hunting. The men had hoped to get food and water at the well outside the Bolling cabin. As Ezekiel ask the men for their help, Nancy quickly made sandwiches of cornbread and pork. Ezekiel got his rifle and he and the men started through the woods.

They were having no luck until Ezekiel spotted a piece of blue ribbon. He told the men what he had taught his girls. As they hurried forward, they found other pieces of blue and green ribbon. Seeing one on a low branch of a tree let the men know which branch of a trail to follow.

It got darker and darker and they had no lights. Ezekiel's heart was breaking until one of the men saw a light through the trees. They got down low and made their way quietly through the bushes to the campsite of the Indians. The Indians had made a large fire and had been cooking something over it.

Ezekiel was horrified to see his girls tied to trees on the far side of the fire. He was more frightened when he realized the Indians were drunk. They were looking at the girls talking and laughing.

Ezekiel and the men backed off a little bit and whispered as they made plans. Ezekiel begged, "Don't do anything rash. They could kill the girls if they knew we were here to take them back."

A noise in the bushes caused the Indians to jump up holding bow and arrows. They crept away from Ezekiel and the men toward the noise. They broke into shrieks and war cries when they discovered a deer in the bushes.

Taking advantage of the Indians being distracted, the three hunters broke into the clearing yelling and shooting. Ezekiel ran to his daughters. Quickly cutting them loose, taking one under each arm, he ran. The Indians, taken by surprise, were so frightened they ran off into the woods. The men ran after Ezekiel and all ran home as fast as they could. Much to their relief, a moon soon came out and helped them to see the trail.

Back at the cabin, the men took the harness off the tired oxen, led them to the barn where they fed the animals and gave them water. Nancy fed all the men and had fresh milk for them. Ezekiel showed the men where they could sleep in the barn.

How joyful the Bolling family was. The girls had acted wisely and remembered what they had been taught. They said the Indians had been good to them and had even given them dried meat to eat.

Ezekiel said, "I guess they meant to raise my girls to work for them and have babies for them. I'm so thankful we found them before they were taken to the Indian village.

Nancy and Ezekiel reminded the girls why they needed to be alert and stay close to home. The girls didn't want to be taken again and maybe never see their family.

THREE WEEKS

When I tell you my story, I know you're going to hide your mouths behind your hands and smirk at each other. I can't blame you. I understand. Whether you want to believe it or not, I'm telling the truth and I'd like to share it with you. Just remember, it **did** happen to my family with no warning, and it could just as easily happen to your family. It was the worst three weeks of our lives. Emily Rand told the ladies in her Sunday School class at their monthly social gathering.

My husband, Bert, is district manager for a software company. We have a fifteen year old son, Michael, and a thirteen year old daughter, Regina. Both children are strong and healthy in both mind and body. They make top grades and are happy in all phases of their lives. I'm telling you this so you won't think of that awful Poltergeist movie and imagine it was teen hormones instead of something more serious. It was hard for me to believe at first, but well ---"

Two years ago we lived in northeastern Virginia in an old historic region and were very pleased with our home, church and social life. Sometimes our son seemed to sleep his life away, but we attributed it to growth spurts.

The first time I noticed a strange occurrence, I was walking past my son's room taking a load of clothes to the laundry room. I heard a voice which grew deeper and louder and then fading as if the person was moving away. I couldn't understand what the person was saying, but something caused me to feel alarm.

I knew my son had gone to his room to study for an exam and had shut his door. I assumed he was alone. I thought a friend might have come over without my knowledge. I knocked on his door and called, but there was no answer and no scurrying of movements. There was an ominous silence as I eased the door open.

Mike was on his bed, on his back, sound asleep with a history book open on his chest. There was no radio or television on. I eased his door shut and went on downstairs thinking it was a man's voice from outside that could be heard through an open window.

Later Regina came bouncing happily into the house. She had been with a friend studying for a literature exam. She called a cheerful greeting and ran up to her room. I heard her scream and then scream again in anger.

Rushing up the stairs, I almost collided with Mike who staggered sleepily from his room after being abruptly awakened. We burst into Regina's room and stopped in shock. Everything that could be moved was out of place. The furniture was cock-eyed all over the room. Stuffed animals were scattered as if they'd been thrown. Clothes had been taken from the closet and were hanging all over the room and on the floor, even from the ceiling fan. How and why had this happened? And why hadn't Mike or I heard anything?

Regina tearfully accused Mike and then quickly realized he would never do this to her. She asked if anyone had been there before she got home. No, I would have known if anyone was in since I had gone past her room while doing chores. Mike and I helped her clean the room and move the furniture back. Boy, was that furniture heavy. How could it have been moved without me hearing it? Bert came home from work and didn't give our story much attention.

During the middle of the morning, around three o' clock, we were awakened by our doorbell ringing and then heard hard, quick knocks on the front door. Hurriedly throwing on robes and slippers, we answered the door.

There stood neighbors from across the street and on either side of us. They were all frightened and concerned.

We invited them in and I fixed hot chocolate while they explained why they were there. Each one told of hearing screams from our house and yells like an Indian might make in movies they'd seen. On man said he thought out house was on fire because he saw flickering flames. The nearer he ran to our house, the less he could see. Running up and peering in the living room window, there was nothing. The neighbors had met each other on our front porch, compared stories and were afraid that someone had broken in and attacked us.

One woman wanted to call the police, but Bert asked what evidence they could produce. He warned them that the police would only be annoyed. We thanked them for their concern and a little after five in the morning, all of us went back to our beds.

Three nights later Bert was out of town on a business trip and our two children were at a basketball game at the school. They were going with some friends, after the game, for pizza. Alone in the house I was sitting up in bed reading and apparently fell asleep. I was awakened by a nauseating odor and loud yells. I jumped out of bed and ran to look in the hall. But I was too frightened to open my bedroom door. I yelled for whoever was out there to go away because I had a gun and would shoot. I also said I had called the police. The yells increased and thumps on my door were frightening. All I could think of was to pray -- and boy did I pray.

As if a switch had been thrown, everything went deadly quiet. I was afraid to leave my room. When Mike and Regina came home they were astonished to see every light in the house was on. I hadn't left my room, therefore, I could not have turned on all those lights. They were shocked to see a crude hand-made hatchet embedded in the outside of my door. Anxiously they pushed my door open and eased in my room fearful of what they would find. I was too frightened to move. How relieved we were to all be together again and safely at that.

The children and I grabbed a change of clothes, toothbrushes and personal items and spent the remainder of the night in a motel. I kept Mike and Regina home from school the next day because we overslept. In the early afternoon we went fearfully back to the house, but nothing had changed. The neighbors had neither seen nor heard anything. They knew how concerned we were because they had witnessed the confusion before.

Later that night Bert came home and was slightly annoyed with us and embarrassed that we had involved neighbors. He thought we were hysterical and overreacting. He accused me of getting the children upset just because I was afraid. When he went up to our bedroom, and saw the hatchet in the door, he began to listen and ask questions. We had a family discussion concerning what had happened to us the night before and what the neighbors had witnessed several days before.

We were late getting to bed. My teenagers went right to sleep. I was the last to go to bed. Bert told me the next morning that he couldn't sleep. There was a noxious odor wafting through the house that disturbed him. A little after midnight he had gotten up to get a drink of water from our bathroom. He leaned over the sink to throw cold water in his face. When he raised his head, his eyes went to the mirror. That's when he got a shock. Standing behind him was an angry, almost nude, Indian with his arms crossed over his chest and glaring as if he were about to attack. When Bert, preparing to defend himself, spun around -- the room was empty. He staggered back to bed and awakened me to tell me what he had seen.

The next morning, after breakfast, we told the children what Bert had experienced. After a family discussion, I suggested that we contact a couple that we had seen on 60 Minutes that were paranormal investigators. The family agreed. That was my task for the day as Bert had to go to work and the children had to go to school. Bert cautioned them to say nothing to anyone until we knew more to tell.

Four days later the couple came and set up all kinds of strange apparatus. It was to be an expensive endeavor but we didn't know what else to do. The couple had two men working the equipment for them while they took notes. They claimed to have evidence of shadow shapes. They suggested that we ask the police if other, who lived there before us, had similar experiences. There was no record at the police station of strange reports.

On Saturday the children and I went to the city library and the librarian showed us microfiche of old newspapers. Twelve years before, a family with four children lived in the house. One night the parents went to a meeting and left a seventeen year old son in charge. He called some friends who came to the house for a party of their own. Word had leaked out and we found out later that some teens had told friends they were coming to crash the party.

When the parents returned a little after eleven, they found dead youngsters all over the house including their own four children. The police closed the house and investigated for days, but no clues were found. There was no evidence of drugs or alcohol, just death. Some of the children had expressions of horror on their faces. No one had lived in the house until we bought it. No wonder we had gotten such a good bargain.

The paranormal experts kept checking and found that about three hundred years before, our five acres was a sacred Indian burial ground. Ghosts? No, I don't believe in ghosts, but we were visited by something or someone who felt we were desecrating their land.

After another family discussion, we agreed to take a loss and give the land to the city with the stipulation that the house would be torn down and no one would live on the grounds again. A lovely park with beautiful landscaped flower beds and fountains were put in. Flowering shrubs bordered the perimeter.

Later we heard that a man had hidden in the bushes waiting for a young woman to come by that he could attack. He was found wandering and babbling about Indians and being whipped with a whip. The city decided that as long as the park was kept peaceful everything would be calm.

This is the gospel truth. 60 Minutes did a segment on it and promised they wouldn't give our names. You can check the records for yourselves. Believe me, today that park is safe and enjoyed by many families. The park was enlarged to include a concrete trail for skaters. A jogging and walking path meanders over the property. A nice playground for small children was put in near the front where everyone could see the children and keep them safe.

We haven't been back, but these are the pictures a friend sent to us. A statue of an Indian has been placed near the center of the park with a pool around it and a fountain. A plaque tells of the Indians who lived there hundreds of years ago and that this was possibly a burial ground.

We moved from Virginia here to Florida. You can rest assured that before we bought our house, we researched it thoroughly. We hope and pray to never get in a mess like that again and hope that no angry spirits followed us.

Thank you for not laughing although a few of you looked relieved. Shall we continue with our program or just have refreshments?

What was that?!!!!

Be Very Afraid

Evil was walking the land and it was so palpable that she could almost taste it in the salty wind blowing up the cliffs from Dead Man's Bay. Imagining that she could hear screams in the wind, she shivered as cold chills tiptoed up and down her spine. Drawing her shawl closer around her shoulders, she quickened her steps on the narrow path at the top of the cliffs.

Dead Man's Bay had always just been called, The Bay, until Cyrus Fletcher took a short cut one night herding his lost sheep home. His widow had explained that she believed he came across the cliffs because it would have taken him about twenty minutes longer to cross the pasture. Too, it was dark and foggy. He had gone to search for eleven lost sheep that had gotten out of the field and wandered off. The local police reasoned that the first sheep had gone over the cliff in the fog and the other sheep followed. Cyrus probably could not see very well in the fog and followed the sheep. The next morning his broken body was found at the foot of the cliffs half in and half out of the water. Most of the sheep had been killed. Others had to be destroyed because of multi injuries. Only one survived. It had landed on the ones that had fallen first.

The moon was mostly behind cloud cover which drifted off every now and then. There was enough light for her to keep safely on the path. Annoyed with herself because her heart was jumping like a Mexican jumping bean, Amelia

Ferguson gave herself a good mental scolding. She was sure she was worried about nothing.

She smiled to herself remembering her Grandfather, Ian Ferguson, and his old time wisdom. He would sit in a rocking chair on the front porch when she brought her worries to him as a twelve year old. He had patted her shoulder and said, "Honey, worrying is like rocking. It's something to do, but it doesn't get you anywhere."

A lot of the older local citizens swore that the cliff path was haunted and that they had seen the ghost of Cyrus Fletcher as well as a woman in a long, white, glowing gown. Amelia comforted herself by speaking aloud. "I don't believe in ghosts, so there. If there are any ghosts around here, just know I don't believe in you and I'm not afraid."

Still speaking aloud, she continued. "Besides if there was a ghost of Cyrus Fletcher, it would mean that he had died a horrible death before his time. That might also mean he had been murdered." She came to a complete stop. "Murdered! That's it. He must have been murdered. But why? And by who? Whom?" she corrected her grammar.

What was that? Was that a footstep in the woods beside the path? Is it a person or some dangerous animal? With her heart hammering so hard that she was finding it difficult to breathe, she began to walk fast and finally broke into a run with gasping breaths. Fear was driving her to a dangerous pace close to the sheer drop. *Is this where Cyrus went over the cliff? Was the woman in white murdered also?*

Spots began to dance before her eyes until she found it next to impossible to focus on the path. Her chest hurt from her labored breathing. Just as she thought she surely would faint from fright, someone ran in the bushes beside her and stretched out an arm to grab her shoulder. Too frightened to make a sound, she struggled to get away and hoped she wouldn't throw herself over the cliff in the meantime. She moaned and gurgled.

"Hush, you fool," a familiar voice spoke harshly in a whisper. "Keep your voice down. I'm trying to watch some people that I think are criminals. If they hear you, they'll know someone is up here and either we'll be in serious trouble or they'll run and I won't be able to apprehend them."

"I'm sorry, Sheriff," she said with relief. "I was thinking of the ghost of Cyrus Fletcher and the woman in white when I heard noises in the bushes. I didn't know it was you. I thought I was a goner for sure."

"Speak softly. What are you doing on the cliff path after dark, or any time? No sensible people travel this way especially after the sun goes down.

"I stayed too long visiting Martha Bennington and needed to get home in a hurry. I thought taking a short cut would get me home sooner. You know, Sheriff, I think Cyrus Fletcher was murdered. I don't know why or by whom, but it makes sense. I'll tell you why." She proceeded to tell him her theory.

"I'll tell you a secret," he said. He had known Amelia all her life and had married her cousin, so he trusted her. "Cyrus Fletcher's case is still open in our books because no one was satisfied with the story we got. Cyrus was born here and grew up here. He had lived in Maine all of his sixty-four years and he was not a careless man. He was too savvy to fall over the cliff, even in a fog. His daddy lived to be one hundred six and his mother was ninety-nine when she died. He probably would have lived many more years."

She thought for a moment. "What happened to his widow?"

"She left about six months after Cyrus died. I heard that she collected insurance and sold the farm for a hefty sum. I guess she wanted to go far away from here and from painful memories. I lost track of her. Seems to me I heard that she remarried soon after to that young lawyer who had opened a practice in our town. He was younger, but I imagine they had something in common for him to marry an older woman and one that was as homely as Ethel. Oh, sorry. That was not a gentlemanly thing to say." Sheriff Ian McGregor grinned like a little boy. "But she was fifty-six and he was only thirty-five. Maybe it was all the money she suddenly received."

"The truth's the truth, Sheriff." Biting her lower lip Amelia struggled with her thoughts and speculations. *Did the Sheriff really believe her, or would anyone believe her? But the Sheriff did say the case is still open and they weren't satisfied with the evidence they have.*

"Sheriff," she began aloud in her excitement and then gasped when his big, calloused hand gripped her mouth and jaws. First she struggled and then remembered that he was watching someone. She patted his hand and nodded. He slowly removed his hand and tapped the end of his index finger across he lips. She nodded again.

His warm breath kissed her cheek as he brought his lips close to her ear to whisper. "Someone is just ahead. Stay here and be quiet." He tiptoed on in front of her, surprisingly quiet in spite of the work boots with the steel toes. She held her breath as he quietly pulled a pistol from the under-arm harness and held it close to his side.

Amelia, standing quietly, almost afraid of breathing, could hear low voices nearby and coming closer. She couldn't hear what was being said, but could hear men's voices. Someone snickered and was quickly hushed. They sounded as if they were lifting something heavy or working at something. *What can possibly be going on beside the bay and on top of the cliff?*

"Hold it right there," the Sheriff's commanding voice rang out. A voice began to curse and a shot rang out.

Amelia gasped and dropped to the ground with her hand held over her mouth. *I mustn't make a sound and let them know I'm here or they will shoot me. Oh, the Sheriff should have waited to get some help. I wonder who it is and how many there are. I wonder if the Sheriff has been shot.*

Hearing the sounds of a struggle and more profanity, Amelia decided to go back and get some help for the Sheriff. She got up from the ground and tried to hurry with as little sound as possible, but her legs were wobbly from fright. She heard running noises behind her and thankfully found some tall bushes beside the path. She ducked behind the bushes just seconds before two men ran around a curve and down the path.

Waiting a few seconds to see if anyone else came by, she eased from behind the bushes and hurried on down the path. In a short time she came to the edge of a village and was surprised to see a group of men talking together. The street lights had just come on as the natural light slowly left the sky. The men's voices sounded excited, therefore, she cautiously walked on by and pretended that she had not observed them.

Wait. One of those men is a deputy. He could help the Sheriff. No! Be careful. You don't know who else is in that group. Those men who ran by you on the path could be there with them.

Amelia was shocked to hear Deputy Mark Polk make a sound like a hiss and say, "Well, he should have kept his nose out of it. I didn't know he was going to do that or I would have warned you guys."

Oh mercy. The Deputy is one of the law breakers. What can I do? I don't know what has happened to the Sheriff and he does need help. I'll risk it and go down to his office.

Amelia walked slowly on by hoping the men would not realize she had heard them talking. Her heart was pounding so hard that she was sure they could hear it.

"Hey, Amelia."

She drew a shaky breath when she heard a neighbor, Ben Goodson, call out to her. Trying to keep from gasping, and showing she had heard the group of men, she turned and smiled at Ben. The deputy and four other men were standing behind Ben. Apparently he had been part of the group.

"Hi, Ben," she called as calmly as she could. "Have you been out of town? I haven't seen you for a while." He took a few steps toward her and she saw the other men relax and turn away.

"Yeah. My uncle, over in Buford County, broke his leg and I went over to help my aunt with the animals and the farm for a few days. She's hired a couple to stay with them so I could come home. What are you doing here?

It's late. Did you just come off the cliff?"

"I'm running some errands for mother and if I don't get moving she'll be worried about me. Good to see you, Ben." She hurriedly walked away.

Amelia walked on to a ladies dress shop owned by a friend of her mother's. She could see that it was closing. As she faced the door of the shop, she glanced back to see where Ben was. He was standing watching her. She quickly ducked into the store.

As the owner closed and locked her door, two late customers walked out before her. Amelia left with them smiling as if she had a conversation going. She glanced to her left glad to see Ben was gone. She excused herself and hurried across the street and down a couple of doors to the middle of the block to City Hall. The Sheriff's office was in the back of this building.

In a small town, everyone knows everyone who is a resident. She knew all of the deputies and now was wondering if she could trust any of them. Amelia said a silent prayer and decided to take a chance.

The woman on duty at a front desk, greeted her. "Well, hello Amelia.

What brings you here?"

"Hi, Marcie. Is the Sheriff in?"

"No, he's out on patrol. Is there something I can do for you?"

"Who's in charge when the Sheriff isn't around?"

Deputy Bill Owens is next in command," she answered, looking perplexed. Amelia knew Marcie was wondering why a sixteen year old girl would be looking for the Sheriff and right at dark.

"May I talk to Bill Owens?"

"Sure. I'll call him."

Marcie made a call to one of the private offices. "He'll be right out," she said with a smile and curiosity written all over her face.

Instead of sitting down, Amelia casually walked to the window and looked out. If Mark or Ben or any of the men in the group had followed her, she needed to have a good story ready that had nothing to do with the cliff.

She jumped guiltily when Bill Owens spoke to her. She whirled around to find him standing close behind her. Whew! He'd gotten too close and she was too occupied with her thoughts to hear him. She told herself to be more cautious and alert.

"Hello, Bill," she answered. "I have something to urgently discuss with you. May we go somewhere private where we can talk?"

"Sure," he said with a slight frown. As they walked by Marcie, she, too, looked curious and puzzled.

Bill stepped aside to allow Amelia to walk in the door ahead of him, shutting the door behind him. "Please, have a seat." He walked over to sit behind a desk in a leather swivel chair. "Now what's so important?"

She leaned over and spoke a little above a whisper. "Do you know where the Sheriff is right now?"

"The exact spot? No. I just know he was going out to walk around town and do a last patrol before he went home. Why?"

Amelia was afraid of being heard. She stood up and walked over in front of him, talking very low. "Can I trust you? Are you a good, clean officer?"

She gasped at her own stupidity.

Bill laughed and lowered his own voice when he realized her expression was serious and fearful. "Well, yes, Amelia. You can trust me and I'd like to think I'm one of the good guys."

"You need to go to the top of the cliff and hurry. The Sheriff had a gun battle up there with some law breakers and he might be hurt. I don't have time to tell you the whole story. Just go up there, but please don't tell anyone I'm the one who told you about this. And, oh please, don't take Deputy Mark Polk with you and don't tell him where you're going. I'll tell you why later. Just hurry."

"Amelia! Are you serious?"

Bill jumped up when Amelia broke into wrenching sobs. He had known Amelia all of her life and knew she was not one to cry or complain. Neither would she try to get attention for herself and cause trouble. He hesitated a moment and then ran out of the room. "Harry! Alex! Come with me. Make sure you're armed and hurry." The three deputies jumped on motorcycles and roared off up the street.

Amelia walked by Marcie without speaking even though Marcie called out to her asking what was going on. Amelia was naturally fair-skinned, but now she was very pale. Her blue eyes were wide with fear and her bow-shaped mouth was drawn tight. Her light brown hair swung in waves below her shoulders. Barely five-four and one hundred four pounds, she looked even smaller as she rounded her shoulders and folded her arms across her middle. She first drug her feet and then walked rapidly to her home at the base of the cliff.

"Amelia, where in the world have you been? I've been worried and when it got dark and you still were not here I --" Her mother looked closely at Amelia and stopped talking to walk over and hug her.

"Something's wrong. What is it?"

Amelia told her mother all that she had experienced. As she talked she grabbed her mother's hands, holding on tight, and grew pale and breathless.

"Honey, I know you've been frightened, but Sheriff Short is capable of doing his duty. He was an M P in the Army and is a sharpshooter. Please calm down and let's eat supper. We'll hear any news by morning, if not sooner."

Amelia prepared to set the table and help get the food ready for them to eat. She was not calmer inside, but she didn't want to make her mother feel worse, so she tried to talk as if she wasn't thinking of the past few hours.

She was preparing for bed when a firm knock sounded on the door. Amelia gasped and grabbed a robe to put on as she hurried to the door. Her mother called for her to wait and they'd go together.

As the heavy knock sounded again, Martha opened the door. "My goodness, what's the rush? Why are you at my door this late at night?"

Mark Polk stood there with an expression like a thunder cloud. He looked over Martha's should at her daughter. "Amelia, what did you tell Bill Owens? I don't know where he has gone and I can't find the Sheriff. What do you know about it?"

"Me?" she squeaked. "Why should I know anything about law business in this town?"

"Well, Marcie said you came in to talk privately to Bill and he ran out with Alex and Harry. I don't know where they are and the Sheriff isn't in town making his rounds. I'm the only one left in case we have any trouble." He was glowering at Amelia and Martha as if they had committed a crime.

"Mark Polk," Martha spoke firmly, "are you saying that we are supposed to know what happens in this town? I don't think so. If Amelia wanted to talk to Bill, I guess that's her business. It's late, now good night." She pushed the door so forcefully that Mark had to step back while Martha closed the door in his face.

When Amelia started to speak, Martha put a finger to her lips and motioned for them to go on up to their bedrooms. She wasn't sure whether Mark had left or whether he could hear them talking downstairs.

"Amelia, there's no need to lie, just talk around the subject just as I did if he tries to talk to you tomorrow. Keep reminding him you're only sixteen and not a deputy. If he persists, ask him if he is implying that he needs you to help do his job."

Amelia had to snicker at her mother as she vehemently gave instructions to Amelia. Martha didn't want Amelia to know how worried she was, so she talked as if she had everything under control.

"Now, let's get into bed, say our prayers and have a good night's rest. What will be, will be. Sheriff Joshua Short is perfectly capable of taking care of the business of this town."

They each went to their rooms. Amelia said a prayer for the Sheriff and the men working with him. Martha did the same but added a plea for God to protect her daughter and give her wisdom to know how to handle the situation.

Amelia could hardly sleep for worrying and was up earlier than usual. She first started coffee and then making biscuits and frying ham. She scrambled eggs and poured orange juice. Saying a silent prayer as she set the table, she got the blackberry jam and butter out of the refrigerator and set them on the table. She almost burned herself taking the biscuits out of the oven when a loud knock came at the front door.

Who could be out this early and why would they be here? She looked up the stairs apprehensively as she slowly started toward the door. Pulling the sash around her robe tighter around her waist, she opened the door a crack leaving her foot against the door so it could not be pushed open against her.

"Hello, Amelia. I'm sorry to be so early, but I saw your light on and knew one of you would be up. May I come in?"

"Of course, Sheriff. Excuse me, but I haven't dressed yet. We generally eat breakfast and then clean up."

"Amelia! There's no need to give your life history. Good morning Joshua. Please join us for breakfast."

"Oh, I can't do that. I didn't mean to be a bother; I just thought you would like to know about last night," he said with a smile as he laid his broad-brimmed hat on the sofa. "I know there's no man in the house and thought you might be relieved to know the outcome of my surveillance."

"We sure will be glad to hear your news. I insist that you eat with us while we talk. I bet you had very little sleep and no breakfast." Martha took his arm and walked into the dining room.

Amelia had already set another place and poured coffee for her mother and Joshua. She brought in a platter of ham and one of biscuits. She went back to the kitchen to get the eggs that she had scrambled for all of them.

"I feel very honored," Joshua smiled, "to share breakfast with you. Amelia, I wanted to thank you for sending the three deputies to help me. It so happened that I really needed them. Three of the men got away, but we now know who they are because the four that I caught, told everything to try to make it easier on themselves."

"I heard a shot, Sheriff. Were you hurt?"

"No, Amelia. The shot came mighty close to my head but no one got hurt except for some bruises when we had to pin them down. Ummm. Pardon me, but this is so delicious, I'd rather eat and talk later. Who made these light as air biscuits? They are so good, they taste almost like cake."
"Amelia cooked the entire breakfast. She's developing into an excellent cook and baker," Martha told him proudly.

"Well, Amelia, I guess we'll lose you before long to some lucky fellow. Any man would be fortunate to get you.

I know both of your parents, or rather knew your father, and I know how well you've been raised."

"Sheriff, that's kind of you to think well of my efforts to cook, but I intend to get a college education before I even think of settling down."

"I'm so happy to hear you say that. Too many of our young people jump into marriage thinking it's going to make a big, happy difference in their lives. And it does for a short time. Then they face reality. Daily expenses for food, clothing, utilities, then taxes, insurance and all the trials and troubles that responsibilities of marriage brings. They are just not mature enough to grow with the responsibilities."

"Let's go into the living room and talk. Amelia, we'll clean up later. Joshua, would you like another cup of coffee to take with you?"

"Please. I'm ashamed of myself for eating so much, but those biscuits are the best I've eaten. Amelia, I'd marry you myself if I weren't too old for you." he laughed.

"Well," Martha stated firmly, "you are too old for her and it doesn't need to be discussed. I thought you came to tell us what happened last night."

"Yes. Let's all sit here where we can talk." Martha and Amelia sat on the sofa holding hands and the Sheriff sat in a lounge chair opposite them.

He began. "Amelia, when I left you on the mountain last night, I was worried that you would be discovered and hurt, or killed. I was so relieved to find that you made it home safely."

"Now. I found several men trying to empty a boat of items, which later turned out to be stolen items from stores and houses. They were valuable appliances and collections. If I had not stopped them, they would have stored them in one of the caves and goodness knows where the items would have been taken next."

Amelia sat on the edge of her seat. "Did you know the men?

"No, although I had seen a couple of them in town. Thank goodness they're not from our town."

"What happened after you stopped them?" Martha interjected.

"I guess it was surprise and nerves, but one man just fired without really aiming. When he did that, some started running. I lost them, but I did hold the others at gunpoint. Boy! I was surprised and pleased when the deputies came to my aid."

"I'm so glad that the men got there in time to help you. I was so scared and worried that you might be hurt," Amelia told him.

"I sure do appreciate your thoughtfulness. Bill tells me that you were suspicious of Mark. Do you mind telling me why?"

"When I came off the mountain I saw a group of men talking to Mark. As I walked near them I heard Mark say that he hadn't warned them ahead of time because he didn't know that someone would be there. I just assumed that he was talking about the situation you found."

Joshua laughed. "You were right to be careful, however, Mark was talking about something very different and certainly not dangerous. You can trust Mark. None of my deputies knew the men that we captured. The ones we caught must be new in the business because they were so willing to spill what they knew in hopes that I would go easy on them."

"What's going to happen to the men you captured?" Martha asked.

"I called Sheriff Ira Stone, in the next county, and he had heard some of the names. He's coming here today to meet the men and see what information he can get from them. He's investigating break-ins where computers, new and used, radio phones and all kinds of electrical equipment were stolen along with expensive cameras and other items."

"Have you caught the men who ran?"

"My deputies are after them now --- including Mark. I'm hopeful that we'll have all of them before this day is out. Well ladies," he stood and reached for his hat, "thank you again for a delicious breakfast and the most delightful company anyone can have."

Martha walked to the door with him after telling him he was welcome any time. Amelia noticed the expression on her mother's face and the way Joshua kept staring at Martha. *Is it possible they are attracted to each other?*

Martha and Amelia were relieved to hear that all of the thieves were captured and that Sheriff Stone had taken them to be incarcerated and tried in his county where the criminals lived.

"What a relief. I was so scared that the men would come after me or that Mark was one of their gang and would hurt me in some way," Amelia told her mother with a shaky laugh.

Martha hugged her and then stepped back to look straight into Amelia's eyes. "My darling daughter. I'm so proud of you and have a lot of faith in your good common sense, **but** please don't take the shortcut at the top of the mountain by yourself or when there is not enough light to see clearly."

"I promise, Mother. That incident scared me enough, but I'm still concerned that Cyrus Fletcher might have been murdered."

"You can't do anything about it. Please don't talk about it publicly or someone might fear you know more than you do and try to kill you."

"I'll keep quiet and only talk about it to you, Mother."

"Good. Joshua says the act of murder concerning Cyrus Fletcher is still open and quietly being investigated."

"That's good news. I would love to know what is found about his death. Knowing what I know now, I'd say his wife knew more about it than was thought possible."

"Just don't talk about it and maybe get involved with a dangerous person,"

"I promise, Mother. Now I have a question for you."

"I'm waiting. Why do you have that smirky grin?"

"My grin isn't smirky. I've observed something and think -- no, I hope, what the outcome will be."

"Well, tell me. I lost the ability to read minds long ago."

"What's between Joshua and you?"

There was a stunned silence until Martha released a gusty breath. "What! What do you mean, what's between Joshua and me? And he's Sheriff Short to you."

"Don't try to get me side-tracked. I saw how you looked at each other. I just wanted you to know that I approve."

"Well, goody, goody. You approve." Martha looked stern and then burst out laughing. "I will admit that I think Sheriff Short is a gentleman and seems to be a man that can be counted on, but don't forget, I loved your father with my whole heart."

"But daddy's been gone most of my life and you've worked so hard to provide for us. If you and the Sheriff are attracted to each other, go for it."

"I can't *go for it* unless he shows some interest. If he ever does, yes, I'll be interested, too."

Amelia finished cleaning the kitchen and started out of the room. "Mother, if you have the sewing finished that you were doing, I'll deliver it for you."

"Now that I'll take you up on. I finished last night. Take this dress to Bertha Newton and this tablecloth to Marylee Parsons."

"Oh, Mother, I hope you're getting paid enough. This dress is more beautiful than one she could buy in a store and this tablecloth is awesome. You have `embroidered beautiful flowers and birds around the edge of it. This took a lot of work and patience."

"These envelopes, one to each woman, has my fee inside. Collect from them as you deliver or bring the items back until they can pay. I don't want to face any trouble with them holding the items and then not paying."

"I understand and I'll make sure I have your pay before I leave the items."

Amelia picked up the sewing, which was heavier than she thought, and left happily to deliver and collect her mother's fee. Mrs. Newton was thrilled with the beautiful dress

Martha had made and paid immediately. Amelia thanked her and went on down the street to Mrs. Parsons.

"Hello, Amelia. What do you have for me? Oh, let me see." Mrs. Parsons oohed and aahed over the beautiful work that Martha had done.

"I can hardly wait to show this at the dinner party for Herman's boss next Friday night. The ladies will be envious of me. Amelia, I'm very sorry, but I don't have any money now. Tell your mother that I'll pay her when I get the money from my husband."

"That's fine, Mrs. Parsons. It took my mother hours to do such tiny stitches and excellent work. I'll bring the tablecloth back when you let me know that you have your money. Have a wonderful day." Amelia stood up to leave.

"Wait, Amelia. You can leave the tablecloth here and you won't have to carry it back and forth so much."

"Oh, I don't mind. I'll wait to hear from you." Amelia left with Mrs. Parsons still sputtering and protesting behind her.

The nerve of her. She brags about how much money her husband makes and attempts to pass herself off as a great socialite, but she can't pay for delicate, detailed work that she ordered. Amelia smiled to herself. *If she wants the cloth badly enough, she'll have the money in a day or two.*

Sure enough, two days later Joanna Parsons showed up with Martha's money for the delicate work on the tablecloth. "Momma said she thinks the tablecloth is the most beautiful she's ever seen. Here's your money. I'm to take the cloth straight home. Thank you ever so much."

Joanna was usually very shy. She was a pretty girl of fourteen with long, curly black hair and violet eyes. Dimples played in both cheeks all the time but were especially noticeable when she smiled. She was laughing now and Martha couldn't resist hugging her before she took the heavy cloth.

"Thank you, dear, for bringing the money to me. I loved doing the work, but I don't think I'll be doing much more like it. The arthritis in my hands is giving me trouble, so I can't work like I used to. Tell your mother I hope she enjoys using the cloth and will take care to keep it for you in the future."

Giggling shyly, Joanna left to take the cloth home. She couldn't wave back because the tablecloth was draped across both arms.

"Oh, Mother, that is such beautiful work. You didn't tell me that your hands are hurting. I'll try to do more work around here and help you all that I can."

"Bless you, darling, I appreciate your help, but I'm not down for the count yet. I may not be able to do such tiny stitches again, but I can still sew. My work has kept food on our table and a roof over our heads for a long time."

The next day Amelia was hanging washed clothes on a line in the back yard. She was singing softly and feeling so good in the warm sun light. The various birds were singing and talking in the trees around her and a saucy squirrel flipped a bushy tail at her as he ran across the yard.

"Miss." Amelia turned to see a little boy about eight years old standing behind her.

"Well, hello. Where did you come from? I didn't hear you come up."

"You wuz a singin so pritty, I din't wana bother you."

"That's all right. Why are you here?"

"A man gived me a whole quarter to brung this to you. You air Amelia ain't you?"

"Yes. Thank you," she reached to take the envelope from him. She laughed to herself when he turned and ran as hard as he could. Opening the envelope she read the short message inside. Turning white as a sheet, she staggered into the house calling to her mother. Martha came walking rapidly when she heard Amelia's croaking cry.

"What is it, darling? Are you sick? Are you hurt?"

Amelia shook her head and sat quickly in a kitchen chair as she handed the paper to her mother. Martha looked carefully at Amelia to see if she looked like she had a fever and then glanced at the message. She gasped and read it again.

Walking to the telephone she called the Sheriff's office. "I need to speak to the Sheriff now," she stated firmly. "Oh, this is Martha Ferguson. I need to speak to Sheriff Short, please. It's an emergency. Tell him to come to my house as soon as possible. No, I don't want to speak to anyone else. The Sheriff already knows about this situation and I need to talk to him. Thank you."

"Mother, the note said to not tell the police."

"Amelia, we will not give in to bullies or any other criminal. Sheriff Short needs to see this and will know how to handle it."

Martha read it slowly out loud. "Missy, you've stuck yore nose where it had no bizness. Ifen you tell who you seen or what you know, it'll be yore funeral. Got it?"

Martha made tea and placed some fresh scones and clotted cream with homemade strawberry jam on the table.

"We'll have a bite to calm us and the Sheriff will enjoy some, too."

Amelia was too upset to eat, but her mother kept talking and urging her until she picked at a still warm scone. Martha and Amelia had each eaten a scone when a heavy knock sounded at the front door. Martha ran to the door and came back into the dining room with the Sheriff. Without saying a word, she handed him the message. He read silently.

"Who was this addressed to?"

Amelia haltingly told him how the envelope was delivered.

"Amelia, do you have any idea what this is referring to?"

"No. Honestly I don't." She put her head down on her folded arms and began to cry. Martha jumped up and sat beside her to hug her.

"What are you going to do, Sheriff?

"We can't rush into anything because we don't know who is responsible for this, nor do we know what he's referring to."

"I wish I had a clue," Amelia sobbed.

Joshua stood and held his hat against his chest. "I'm taking this to go over it with a fine tooth comb. Maybe the wording will give us a clue as to who is talking. I'll do the best I can, Amelia. In the meantime don't go anywhere alone. Call me if you get an idea."

Martha walked him to the door. Amelia could hear them talking low to each other but she couldn't hear what they were saying.

Two miserable weeks went by. Martha and Amelia were beginning to feel as if nothing would be done about the threatening message. On a Friday afternoon the Sheriff came with a big grin on his face.

"You know something!" Amelia cried out.

"Yes. I began to think it was a useless investigation until a man got anxious and gave himself away."

Martha sunk into a chair in the living room looking pale and worried. "Well, for goodness sakes, tell us. This has been a miserable two weeks."

"It's very simple," Joshua smiled. "Amelia, remember on the top of the mountain when you hid as the men ran by you?"

"Oh, yes, and I was so scared."

"One man had seen you there but didn't know you. He was more concerned with getting down off the mountain before I came back up. Then you went on down and saw a group of men talking. One of those men was a deputy of mine."

"Yes, I remember. I was suspicious of him at first."

"Well, you were right to be suspicious. Although Mark Polk was not one of the criminals, he knew what they were doing and covered with them in exchange for a small sum of money."

"What is being done about the threatening message sent to Amelia?" Martha was anxious and angry.

"Mark Polk has turned state's witness in exchange for not being charged and will have to turn in his badge and gun. He'll no longer be a deputy. He gave me the names of the men involved that I hadn't caught yet. None of them will bother you, Amelia."

Amelia went to her bedroom to lie down. She was feeling weak and shaky. She did not feel relief for several days.

Three months later Amelia served as a maid of honor in the wedding of her mother and Sheriff Short. She followed her new stepfather's advice to be very afraid and not go near the place where stolen items were stored.

DEATH IN THREE QUARTER TIME

Ziggy Martin was one of the best jazz musicians on Bourbon Street in New Orleans. He could be heard playing the piano out on the street and hundreds of people crowded into the bar and restaurant to hear him play.

Alethia, his wife, was very proud to be linked with him and felt he could be famous and bring in big money if he went to other places to play. Ziggy was not as interested in the money as he was in knowing he pleased people.

Ziggy's real name was William Henderson Martin. When he was two, a man had asked him his name and he had solemnly looked up and said, "Ziggy." He had been called Ziggy every since then.

Alethia wanted to leave New Orleans. The hurricane and flooding had left it mostly empty which meant there was not much money being made.

This particular Saturday night the place was too crowded for people to be comfortable. The air was heavy with smoke, odors of alcohol and body odors. There were an unusual number of tourists. Not much money.

The musicians in the band were uncomfortable in the heat of the room with no fresh air stirring. Perspiration ran down their faces down their necks and down on their body. Their skin itched with the drying sweat and the crowded conditions. They finally walked off the floor and left Ziggy playing as if he were in a trance.

Although the tip glass had only a small amount in it, free drinks were plentiful. Ziggy fumbled for a glass while continuing to play with one hand. Alethia said, "Wait, honey, I'll help you with that." She almost dropped the glass as she handed it to him.

The crowd went into a frenzy of clapping, whistling and yelling when Ziggy stopped playing. He sat stiffly and finally fell face down on the keys. A dreadful silence fell over the crowd and then a scream.

"He's dead!"

NOPD came in record time and investigated. The M E was called and he took the body off. Sunday the police were swarming over the place trying to find the last glass Ziggy had drunk from. The evidence pointed to poisoning. The glasses had been picked up and washed. It was a lost cause until one officer noticed the cameras around the room.

Tapes were viewed over and over until a rookie office called out for them to stop at a particular spot. He pointed out that a woman had put something in a glass before she gave it to Ziggy. The woman was Alethia.

She was questioned for hours until she finally broke and confessed. "I wanted him to go somewhere that he would be more appreciated and make more money, but his heart was here in New Orleans. Then I remembered the million dollar policy on him and thought I, at least, could get away.

Needless to say she got away all right. Life in prison.

COLLECTIONS BY SIOUX

All of the short stories are my original ones, kookie thoughts and all. These tidbits following my stories are simply items I've collected over the years. These are not my work; sorry, I don't know the authors, or originators, but I'd like to share them.

The average man, to get by these days, has to be something of a contortionist. He has to keep his back to the wall and his ear to the ground. He's expected to put his shoulder to the wheel, his nose to the grindstone, keep a level head and both feet on the ground. At the same time, he must look for the silver lining with his head in the clouds -- to say nothing of keeping his eye on the ball.

* * * * *

Volunteers are like:
FORD -- they have better ideas
COKE -- they're the real thing
PAN AM -- they make the going great
PEPSI -- they've got a lot to give
DIAL soap -- they care more; don't you wish everyone did?
FROSTED FLAKES -- they're grrrrreat!

* * * * *

When you're feeling down, just think of the teakettle. When it is up to its neck in hot water, it still sings.

* * * * *

A lot of men would like to see their wives wearing their dresses longer; about a year longer.

* * * * *

One reason a dog is so loveable is because its tail wags - not its tongue.

* * * * *

Worry is interest paid on trouble before it is due.

* * * * *

Your ulcers are not due to what you're eating, but to what's eating you.

* * * * *

The most important thing about your lot in life is whether you're using it for building or for parking.

* * * * *

Blessed are the flexible for they shall not be bent out of shape.

* * * * *

Almost anything in life is easier to get into than to get out of.

* * * * *

Health insurance is like wearing a hospital gown -- you only <u>think</u> you're covered.

* * * * *

A great actor can bring tears to your eyes, but so can a mechanic.

* * * * *

I haven't caught up with yesterday yet. By tomorrow I should be ready for today.

* * * * *

Wit is something to treasure, charm is something to live, peace is something to keep, love is something to give.
Joy is something to feel, trust is something to find, God is the one to thank from now until the end of time.

* * * * *

The World Is Mine

The other day upon the bus I saw a lovely girl with golden hair. I envied her, she was so lively, and wished I was as fair. When she rose to leave I saw her hobble down the aisle. She had one leg, and used a crutch, and as she stood, a smile. Oh, God, forgive me when I whine; I have two legs, the world is mine.

And then I stopped to buy some sweets; the lad who sold them had such charm. I talked with him, he was so pleased, if I were late, it would do no harm. And when I left he said, "Thank you. You've been so kind. It's nice to talk with folks like you. You see, I'm blind." Oh, God forgive me when I whine; I have two eyes, the world is mine.

Then later walking down the road I saw a child with beautiful eyes of blue. He stood and watched the others play. It seemed he knew not what to do. I paused a moment and said, "Why don't you join the other children, dear?" He looked ahead without a word and then I knew, he could not hear? Oh, God forgive me when I whine; I have two ears, the world is mine.

With legs to take me where I go; with eyes to see the sunset's glow; with ears to hear what I should know, dear, God forgive me when I whine; I'm blessed indeed --- the world is mine.

* * * * *

Six Gifts That Don't Cost a Cent

<u>LISTENING</u>: Let people think you're interested in what they have to say. Really listen. No interruptions, no daydreaming, just listen.

<u>AFFECTION</u>: Be generous with hugs, and any small action that shows you care. Give lots of praise.

<u>LAUGHTER</u>: Share articles, funny stories and jokes. Give greetings that say 'I love to laugh with you.'

<u>WRITTEN NOTE</u>: A thank you, or you did a great job. Let the person know they're appreciated, it could change a life.

<u>A COMPLIMENT</u>: A simple, "That's a good color on you, your food was wonderful, you have a great smile..." that makes everyone feel good.

<u>A FAVOR</u>: Go out of your way to do something nice for someone else. Carry the trash for an elderly person or a home bound sick person. Sweep their driveway or front porch. Take them for a drive or offer to take them to an appointment. Do something for someone that is difficult for them to do for themselves.

* * * * *

And now abideth faith, hope and love; these three but the greatest of these is love. (1 Corinthians 13:13)

* * * * *

Quilt of Holes

As I faced my Maker at the final judgment, I knelt before the Lord along with all the other souls. Before each of us laid our lives like the squares of a quilt in many piles. An angel sat before each of us sewing our quilt squares together into a tapestry that is our life.

But as my angel took each piece of cloth off the pile, I noticed how ragged and empty each square was. They were filled with large holes. Each square was labeled with a part of my life that had been difficult, the challenges and temptations I had faced every day of my life. I saw hardships that I endured, which were the largest holes.

I glanced around me. No one else seemed to have such squares. Other than a tiny hole here and there, the other tapestries were filled with rich color and the bright hues of worldly fortune. I gazed upon my own life and was disheartened. My angel was sewing the ragged pieces together, threadbare and empty.

Finally the time came when each life was to be displayed; held up to the light. The scrutiny of truth. The others rose, holding up their tapestries. My angel looked at me and nodded for me to rise.

My gaze dropped to the ground in shame. I had love and laughter in my life, but there had also been trials of illness and false accusations that took from me, and I had to start over many times. I often struggled with temptation, only to somehow muster the strength to pick up and begin again. I spent many nights on my knees in prayer asking for help and guidance. I had often been held up to ridicule, which I endured painfully. Each time offering it up to my Heavenly Father in hopes that I would not melt within my skin beneath the judgmental gaze of those judging me.

And now, I had to face the truth. I rose and slowly lifted the squares of my life to the light. An awe-filled gasp filled the air. I gazed around at the others who were staring at me with wide eyes.

Then I looked at the tapestry before me. Light flooded the holes creating an image --- the face of Christ. Then our Lord stood before me with warmth and love in His eyes. "Every time you gave to someone in need and allowed Me to work through you it became My life, My hardships and My struggles. Each point of light is when you stepped aside and let Me shine through.